Children of
the
Benin Kingdom

Dinah Orji

Edited by Sonya McGilchrist

www.dinosaurbooks.co.uk

Published by Dinosaur Books Ltd, London
The rights of Dinah Orji to be identified as the
author of this work has been asserted by her in
accordance with the
Copyright, Designs and Patents Act, 1988

ISBN 978-1-9993363-3-2

British Library Cataloguing in Publication Data
A CIP catalogue record for this book is available from the
British Library.

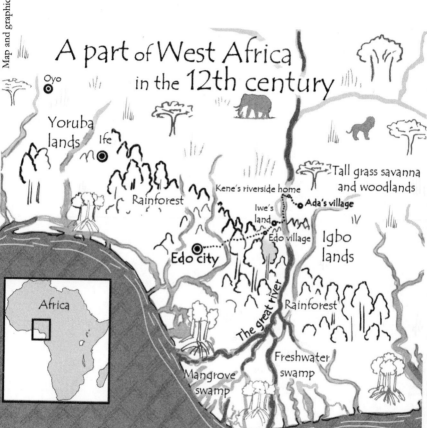

A part of West Africa in the 12th century

Oyo

Yoruba lands

Ife

Rainforest

Kene's riverside home

Ada's village

Iwe's land

Edo village

Edo city

Tall grass savanna and woodlands

Igbo lands

Rainforest

Africa

The great river

Mangrove swamp

Freshwater swamp

Notes:
- The dotted line shows the journey taken by Ada and her friends
- The distance from Ada's village to Kene's riverside home is a full day's walk across open country

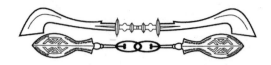

Pronouncing the names in *Children of the Benin Kingdom*

Ada – pronounced *a*-da

Ginika – pronounced ji-*nee*-kah

Eze –pronounced *eht*-zeh

Akele – pronounced ar-*kay*-lay

Mbe – pronounced *mm*-bey

Ujo – pronounced *oo*-jor

Chika – pronounced *chee*-ka

Kene – pronounced *keh*-ne

Madu – pronounced *mah*-doo

Iwe – pronounced *ee*-weh

Amaka – pronounced ah-*ma*-ka

Nosa – pronounced *no*-sa

Itohan – pronounced *ee*-to-han

Uche – pronounced *ooh*-chay

Osawe – pronounced oh-*sah*-wey

Obiro – oh-*bee*-row

Efe – pronounced *eh*-feh

Amenze – pronounced ah-*men*-zay

Prologue

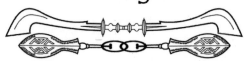

The Benin Kingdom, 12th century...

Akele hid from sight, sheltering beneath the wall at the city's edge.

She gathered her shawl around her shoulders.

It didn't matter that she was a queen. The palace was no longer safe for her.

Ahead stretched open farmland, barely visible through the night rain. And beyond that, the great forest.

"Protect me now, Ogun," she whispered to the god. "And protect my unborn child."

Then she set off, stumbling into the dark.

Her foot slipped in the mud and the rain stung in her eyes, but she kept moving.

The rainforest was her only hope.

For my Mum...
humble, beautiful and full of grace

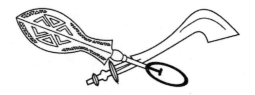

Part
One

Chapter One

A visit from Mama Ginika

Ada was hunting. Above her in the tree the grey bird hadn't even noticed. It was perched on the branch, rubbing its beak and ruffling its feathers. Ada was so nimble that she had climbed all the way up, until she was just an arms-length away.

And she had long arms. Long legs too.

Ada was only ten years old, but already she was the best climber in the village, everyone said it.

She reached out – stealthy as a leopard – c*loser… closer…*

Then suddenly the bird was gone, flitting away with an angry chatter.

"Next time the leopard will get you!" Ada yelled.

And then she grabbed the branch and let herself swing.

****

"What is she doing now?" Mama Ginika tutted.

The old woman watched Ada dangling from the tree at the end of Papa Eze's crop garden, with her toes scuffing the dirt.

Papa Eze didn't look up from his work.

He was preparing a mixture of leaves in water, carefully folding, pressing and pulling them apart.

"She's climbing," he said.

Mama Ginika crossed her arms.

"Well I can see that Papa, but why?"

"She likes climbing. And she's good at it. That branch she's on – she can keep hanging there longer than any of the others."

Mama Ginika shook her head.

"That girl needs a mother."

Papa Eze poured the green liquid into a gourd.

"Drink this when you get home," he said gently. "It has a bitter taste. But you will soon feel well again."

"Thank you," said Mama Ginika. She gave him a cowrie shell.

"There is no need," said Papa Eze, pushing the shell back into her hand.

Then he looked at his daughter, still dangling.

"Why do you think she needs a mother?"

"It is not a criticism," replied Mama Ginika. "You have done a good job Eze, a very good job to bring her up on your own. But can she cook?"

"Cook? We manage," he said. "And she's still learning… "

"She needs to learn quickly. Think about it Eze, if she can't cook, how will she look after a family?"

Papa Eze snorted.

"I'm teaching her plant lore. Tree, plant, and herb medicine. The sacred ways of the forest."

Mama Ginika looked down at a bundle of leaves around Eze's feet.

"The ways of the forest… of course that is a good thing Papa, of course it is. We need your skills."

"I have helped many sick people."

"Yes. But… "

She placed a hand on his shoulder.

"She must fit in with the others. Send her to me and I will teach her, just like I taught my own daughters."

Papa Eze watched the old woman as she walked away. She picked her way between the neatly planted rows of okra seedlings with her walking stick and stopped to speak with Ada.

The little girl dropped down from her tree, greeted Mama Ginika politely, then skipped alongside the old woman to the edge of the village.

And Papa Eze watched his daughter and ran his fingers through his greying beard.

He had done his best, but he knew that he couldn't teach her everything.

****

That evening Papa Eze and Ada walked down to the river below the village. Sometimes they came here, just the two of them, to watch the sun set.

Along the way, Papa Eze knelt down to look at a

small plant growing beside the path.

"Well this is a surprise. Look daughter, see? Golden-leaf. One day, this will be a beautiful tree. It has never grown here before."

Ada leaned forward, hands on her knees.

"Is it good?"

"Oh yes, it is a blessing. Leaves for ailments of the stomach, sticks for cleaning teeth… it has many uses. I've wanted some golden-leaf bark for a while."

He straightened up. "But not this one. Not yet. We must give it a chance to grow tall and strong."

"And we take just what we need, no more," said Ada.

"Exactly so."

They walked on.

"Daughter, do you like Mama Ginika?"

"Oh yes, she's nice. She's very old isn't she?"

"Very old. And I think maybe she needs some help at her home sometimes."

Ada thought about it.

"Could I help her?"

"That would be kind. She has been unwell

recently, but sometimes sickness isn't just in the body, it is in the spirit. Perhaps she needs to spend more time with younger people."

By now they had come to the river's edge and Ada paddled her feet in the water.

"Mama Ginika is very wise," said Papa. "You will learn many things from her, just as she once learned from her mother, and all her ancestors past."

Ada nodded and watched as a tiny fish swam over her toes.

Then she looked up.

"Papa... I want to ask you something."

"Yes?"

"Do *I* have ancestors?"

Eze raised his eyebrows in surprise and for a moment he was lost for words. He laughed.

"You? Of course you do! Dear child, everybody has ancestors."

"Yes Papa – but I have seen you talk to your ancestors in the shrine, asking for advice. And sometimes we offer the palm wine together."

"That's right. We do."

"But... but they are not my ancestors though.

We never talk to my ancestors."

Papa Eze held out his hand.

"Come," he said. "I want to show you something."

****

Papa Eze led Ada through the breadfruit trees behind the village, then turned away from the path. He knelt down beside his daughter and pointed.

"Do you see that stone? The flat one?"

"Yes."

The stone was the colour of amber, lying half buried among the tree roots.

"That belongs to your ancestors."

Ada looked at the stone, and Papa Eze felt her uncertainty.

"I know. We have no carved figures here… it is not a shrine, but your ancestors are watching you still. They are always watching. Watching and protecting. When you were a baby, when I found you, they asked me to put that stone there for you."

Ada nodded. Now she knew what to tell her

friends, next time they asked. The stone belonged to her ancestors…

Then Papa Eze put his arm around her shoulder.

"Come, my daughter. It is time to sleep."

As they walked home he thought: soon I will have to tell her.

****

Papa Eze's first wife and only son had died many years ago, stricken by fever. That had been a terrible time. Long ago now – how long exactly he couldn't remember.

After that he had buried his sadness in his work, and in his study of plants.

He had started taking longer and longer walks, venturing further away from the village in search of new cures and new knowledge, and he became known in the land around for his skill with the healing properties of plants.

But on feast days, when everyone gathered in the village, people would ask him why he didn't take new wives.

Eze would just smile and say he had other things

to think about.

"When the time is right. It is up to the gods."

The villagers would shake their heads, but Eze was kind and generous with his herb lore remedies so they let him be.

And maybe he was right.

Because one day, Eze found Ada.

He had ventured south, to the very edge of the great forest, following the graceful, grazing duiker. He was searching for a certain tree – he knew its bark to be a powerful cure.

Setting off early, he had taken his stick and his bag for carrying whatever he gathered. Over his shoulder he'd slung his knife for cutting branches and stripping bark.

Now, ahead of him, was a tangled path into the forest.

Eze went in search of something rare – and he come back with something precious.

A baby.

****

Eze had come walking into the village – through the thatched round houses where he was now one of the elders – holding the infant wrapped in his cloth bag.

"She is a blessed child," he'd told his curious neighbours. "I found her alone and unprotected. But in all that forest no wild animal had harmed her. No snake, no leopard, not even a biting insect. The ancestors were watching over this child. Now we must do the same."

And because Eze was an elder and much loved by all his neighbours, and known for his kindness, they all agreed and accepted what he said. After all, the child must have powerful ancestors to have survived alone in the forest. They would not want to anger them!

The child would be raised as one of theirs and called Ada.

But the truth about what Eze had really found in the rainforest – what he had really seen that morning – he never told to anybody.

He decided it would be safer for the child if he kept that a secret.

There would be time later, he thought. One day, when Ada was grown up, he could tell her where she really came from.

Chapter Two

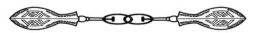

A quest for Ada

"**Y**ou're almost as tall as me, daughter. It's time to stop growing, or you will make me feel small."

Ada laughed.

"But Papa, I *am* as tall as you. And you are small!"

Ada was twelve now, and her smile was the brightest thing in Papa Eze's world. Her long black hair was parted in the middle and neatly arranged into two thick plaits (Mama Ginika had taught her that). She always walked with her head held high.

"Daughter, today I am leaving you in charge of our home. I have an important journey to make."

Ada's eyes brightened.

"Is it a secret?"

Papa Eze looked surprised.

"What makes you say that?"

"Because you haven't told me where you're going."

"Well then," he replied. "Yes. It is a secret."

"Papa!"

But he refused to tell her anything more as he packed his bag with provisions. Ada stood watching him wrap plump bean cakes in a palm leaf.

"I will follow you."

"You can't," he smiled. "You have a job to do."

She frowned.

"What job?"

"It's very hard work. I want you to help Mbe clear away the yam stalks."

Her shoulders slumped.

"That's boring Papa, do I have to? And Mbe is so serious and gloomy. He never laughs."

"Mbe is trying to learn," said Papa Eze. "And he's trying to be helpful."

Mbe was only a year older than Ada but much quieter. His parents had died when he was young, and he had lived with his uncle for a while. But then his uncle's family grew and there was little room for Mbe. Eze had stepped in and offered to take the boy on as an apprentice.

That had been last year. One evening, Eze had looked at Ada as they were eating and told her about his plan.

"His name is Mbe. He needs a new home, and we need some help."

"We don't need help Papa. I can cook now."

"But I'm getting old. And you cannot do everything. We have the crops to keep, and plants to gather – and soon our home will need a new roof…"

Ada shrugged.

"OK. But only if he's nice."

****

Mbe was nice. He worked hard. Every morning he woke early and went to the enclosed land where Papa Eze kept his remedies – the dried leaves tied in bundles, bark strips laid neatly out to dry and earthenware pots containing seeds and roots. Every day Mbe set out matting beneath a large cotton canopy, ready for Papa Eze to sit and speak with anyone who travelled to see him.

Mbe filled the water jugs and laid out dried wood for the fire. Then he would run back to Papa Eze's crop rows, and begin work before the day grew hot, raking out weeds and preparing new beds for planting.

****

"I would help him myself," continued Papa Eze. "But I have my important journey to make."

"Your secret journey you mean. That's the only reason you want me to stay with Mbe. And be bored," Ada said.

"Correct," replied the old man. "And Mbe is not boring. He's just bored of waiting for you. Now hurry up child."

Papa Eze looped his bag over his shoulder and took up his stick. He embraced his daughter and set off. Ada watched him making his way along the path through the village.

****

Mbe was already half done with the yam plot. He'd dug up the old stems from last season and was preparing the ground, ready for the new planting.

He looked up and smiled as Ada joined him. She started working at the far end of the row.

As she dug at the earth, she was thinking about finding the golden-leaf with Papa.

And she remembered what he had said – how he had been wanting some of its bark for a while...

She had noticed, recently, that Papa sometimes walked with a limp. And sometimes, when he thought nobody was looking, he rubbed at his hip.

Maybe he had an illness, and needed the bark to cure himself?

Ada looked at Mbe, gathering up another heap of cut stalks to carry away.

And suddenly she had an idea.

Back at the herb store she checked through Papa's bundles of leaves and plants, some dried and stacked, some growing fresh and neatly tended, marked out with stones.

But no golden-leaf bark. None that she could see anyway...

Papa would be so pleased if she could fetch

some for him.

****

Mbe frowned, uncertain.

"Really. It won't take us long," Ada continued. "And we can finish this when we get back."

"But Ada, how far is it?"

"We go straight south. We'll be back before nightfall."

Still Mbe didn't move.

"Papa will be pleased. He'll see how clever we are."

Reluctantly, he laid down his hoe.

"You're sure it's not far?"

"Not if we walk fast."

Ada ran into the house to pack food and drink for the journey, just as Papa had done a short while earlier.

When she'd finished, Mbe was already waiting – standing at the end of the garden, leaning on a spear and watching the path out of the village. Seeing the weapon, Ada instinctively checked for her knife.

Mbe was right of course. On such a journey they might need to protect themselves.

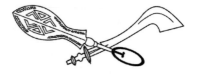

Chapter Three

Divination

E ze had made good speed at first.
He had climbed the hill outside the village and crossed the land beyond, where young men were watching the cattle.

Then he passed Mama Ginika's house. The old woman had been pounding yam in the shade beside her door.

Papa Eze had continued on, joining the main track towards the west. It was a clear line stretching away through the grass, trodden for generations by cattle and people.

A long day's journey lay ahead. But today he wanted answers, and there was only one man he could think of to ask.

The sun was past midday and Eze was limping by the time he saw what he was looking for – a great grey rock, some distance from the track.

The ache in his right hip was slowing him down. He rested, leaning on his staff. The old man thought briefly about what plants he might use to help with his ache. But then he shook his head and sighed.

His suffering came from a deeper cause.

It had been growing steadily and each season, as his daughter grew taller, the pain got worse. He had always been careful to hide it from her.

Many of the cures that he used to treat others, he gave to himself.

They helped for a while.

But finally – reluctantly – Papa Eze decided to seek the help of another. The only other man said to have as much skill with healing as himself.

While Eze used his herb lore to treat illness, this man, it was said, understood the spirit world.

Ujo. The diviner.

****

The great rock loomed up directly ahead and as Eze approached a figure appeared, silhouetted against the sky.

Eze felt a gloom pressing down on him.

The path to the top was narrow and stony. Halfway up, it also became a roadway for termites, and Eze found himself following the same course as countless numbers of tiny creatures, a black river of life flowing out and back again, carrying food to a towering nest somewhere far below.

In happier days he might have followed them, just to see where they went. There were always things to be learned.

But today, he had no time. Their paths separated and Eze struggled on upwards.

****

"You seek answers?"

The man was thin, gaunt almost. Eze studied him and was surprised to see how much he had aged in the years since they had last met. His hair was sparse and grey, his cheeks sunken.

There was nothing special about him, thought Eze, nothing to mark him out as one who spoke with spirits – except for his eyes perhaps. They were still piercing, set deep under heavy brows. For a moment Eze felt himself unbalanced by their gaze.

But he settled his grip on his walking stick and recovered himself.

"Yes, I have questions," he replied. "Whether or not you can answer them."

The man smiled and Eze saw that his teeth were stained dark.

"Of course I can answer them," he said. "Herb master."

Then he turned without speaking and crossed the flat top of the great rock.

Eze followed.

****

The diviner ducked down and pushed aside the ragged cloth that covered the doorway to his small home. Leaning on his stick, Eze followed.

It took a moment for Eze's eyes to adjust to the gloom. The clay walls were crumbling and not properly repaired – or even patched-up – after previous rains. Opposite the door, a cobweb stirred restlessly in a crack that gaped through to the outside, letting in a muffled light.

The room was plain, with barely space for two to sit comfortably.

Ujo was already sitting, unwrapping a cloth parcel. He spoke softly to himself, as he lifted the diviner's tool within – the four strands, tied with seed pods, that would be cast on the ground in search of meaning.

Eze glanced past him to the twigs and dried leaves stacked against the wall – there was nothing here that he didn't use himself, and he knew that many of these plants had more power when they were fresh cut. There was little point in storing them like this…

He turned back to the diviner, almost making up his mind to leave. Perhaps this journey had been a mistake.

But he found those eyes fixed on him again. And Ujo began speaking.

"You are in pain," he said. "Because of the secret you are hiding."

Chapter Four

Lost

"No – I remember now! It's this way…"

Ada changed direction again, leading Mbe up a tangled bank beside a river channel. They had been searching all morning, scanning the horizon for any sign of the golden-leaf tree.

The day had grown hot, and Ada had begun to feel tired. And cross with herself. She felt suddenly childish for leading Mbe out here on this wild search, instead of staying at home to do the job she'd been told to do.

Mbe kept following her without complaining – and his patience only made Ada feel more annoyed.

"I know it grows here somewhere…" she said again.

She scrambled to the top of the bank, grabbing

fistfuls of grass to help herself up.

She stood up straight – and the breath caught in her throat.

"Look!"

From up here, they had a clear view over the tops of the reed beds. In front of them was open grassland dotted with trees, the same as it was behind. But not far to the south was the great forest.

It lay ahead of them like a dark wall.

Mbe reached her side.

"We should not be here," he whispered. "The forest is dangerous."

But Ada could see the wonder and curiosity in his eyes as he too stared towards the trees.

"I came here once with Papa. It's not dangerous. Not if you're careful."

Mbe glanced behind him.

"I think we should go back."

But Ada was already scrambling down the bank ahead, splashing through the water.

"Come on!"

Mbe scrambled down too. He paused at the

water's edge to refill his gourd, then he hurried after her.

When he caught up with her again, she was crouching down in the undergrowth signalling for him to keep quiet.

"Look!" she hissed. "Duiker!"

"Is that good?"

"Yes – Papa told me they like to eat golden-leaf leaves. We might be close."

Mbe glanced around again, then gripped his spear.

"Come on then Ada. Let's look. But then we must get home."

The duikers scattered as Ada and Mbe approached – and then Ada let out a whoop and started running.

"I was right! This is it."

Mbe ran up beside her.

"Really?"

"Yes!"

She was already at work with her knife, pulling at a low branch of the tree and stripping bark and leaves from one side.

"Not too much," she said. "We only take what we need."

Mbe held the end of the branch for her and watched.

"Will it help Papa Eze a lot?"

"I hope so," she nodded. "We came for it once when a neighbour was very sick."

She wrapped some leaves and bark in her bag. Then she looked at him.

"Thank you for coming with me."

But Mbe wasn't listening. He was staring past her. "Men!"

****

Edo. The forest people.
Ada and Mbe stood frozen in fear as three figures emerged from the trees, close enough to call out to. They were tall and strong, with red wrappers. One carried a bow, the other two had curved swords hanging from leopard skin belts.

They stood staring out across the open land for a moment until one of them pointed. Then they turned to look at the river where it flowed into the trees.

If they had spotted the children, they showed no sign of it.

Now, as Ada and Mbe watched, a boat came into view, gliding towards the armed men. It was a long, low canoe, steered by two men and loaded down with goods.

Voices reached them – words in Edo, hard to understand.

The canoe paddled onwards, beneath the canopy of the trees, and the men followed.

As soon as the forest men were out of sight Ada and Mbe started running, scrambling up the steep bank and sliding down the other side into the long grass.

And as they ran, they were laughing.

****

It was almost dark when the children got back to the village. Mbe walked with Ada to the edge of the yam plot and watched as she went to find Papa Eze.

Then he walked across to his own small home.

It had been built for him by all the villagers at the end of the last rainy season.

In just a few weeks they had made it for him, young and old working together – treading the earth with their feet to make good clay for the walls, gathering and bundling the thick ata grass for the thatched roof; and at the end of each day everyone eating together by the fire, with Papa Eze laughing, telling stories and passing around palm wine.

Eventually a neat, circular structure with red clay-earth walls, and a well-knit, conical thatched roof had grown up out of the ground.

******

Inside, Mbe lay down on his mat to sleep. He pictured the Edo men they had seen earlier.

Before he'd come to live with Papa Eze he had dreamed of escaping to a new life. On his loneliest days he had even dreamed of what it might be like in the great Edo city in the forest.

Everyone had heard stories about the Edo sky-king – the great Ogiso! The ironsmiths and other tradespeople brought tales of the fabulous kingdom whenever they came to into the village.

Mbe had listened, entranced.

There would be good work, clearing space in the forest, digging ditches, building walls, farming new land. For a while Mbe had dreamed of such a life, imagining how it would feel to be a part of a great kingdom.

Mbe used to think about that all the time.

But that dream seemed less important now.

He liked helping Papa Eze and knowing that he really belonged somewhere. He liked growing things and learning about the secrets of all the plants. And he liked Ada.

Chapter Five

Treasure
in the earth

Ada unwrapped the precious bundle of golden-leaf and went to tell Papa what she had found.

But there was no sign of him.

She checked the store room. Everything was in its proper place. Then she went to the household shrine where she knelt down in front of the carved wooden figures of Papa Eze's ancestors; all the past generations who watched over them. For as long as Ada could remember, these figures had been a part of her life.

"Protect Papa Eze tonight. Guide him safely home… and don't let him be cross with Mbe for leaving the crops for one day."

Ada remembered to leave a gift at the shrine — a small handful of palm kernels – then went to look outside.

She followed the path through the village, past the evening chatter of neighbours, and a sudden thought came to her. She changed course and hurried across to the hidden grove that Papa Eze had once shown her.

Perhaps seeing the stone would help her feel less worried — the amber coloured stone given by her own ancestors.

****

Ada stood quietly at the edge of the grove, dusk behind her, total blackness ahead.

Were her ancestors watching her here? She felt her heart racing.

She knelt, and reached forward.

The stone must have been lighter than it looked — or maybe Ada was pulling it harder than she realised – because suddenly it shifted.

She gasped.

Even in the gloom she could see what had

happened. The stone had moved forward and tipped up.

She stared, suddenly appalled at what she'd done. She was not even supposed to be here…

Ada pulled desperately at the stone, trying to set it straight again. But her hand brushed into the space beneath it – and she felt something.

Something hidden under the stone.

Unable to stop herself, Ada reached further in – and her fingers wrapped around something hard and curved. She drew the object out to hold it up in the moonlight.

And stared.

Even in this darkness, glinting in the moonlight, she could tell that it was the most strange and beautiful thing she had ever seen.

What was it? It had hard, fine edges, like the bark of a young iroko tree. How was it even possible to create something so fine?

She turned it over in her hands, marvelling at it.

Where had it come from?

And then a shadowy figure, its head hooded beneath a large cloth, stepped out from the bushes behind her.

Ada froze, too startled even to move, as the figure reached out to her: an open hand, gesturing for the treasure.

And again she could not stop herself. She gave the thing up.

And in a moment it was gone. The hooded figure wrapped it in folds of cloth.

"This should not be seen…"

The voice was a whisper, a sound like a night breath in the leaves.

The figure knelt beside her and bowed towards the stone.

"What does this mean, beloved ancestors? Why did you bring this child here like a thief in the night? Why did you tempt her to lift the stone?"

Suddenly Ada heard her own voice, small in the darkness.

"I… I should not have done it…"

There was silence for a moment, before the figure spoke again.

"Perhaps. But I do not think that is true."

The head turned, the cloth covering fell away and

Ada found herself looking into her Papa's eyes.

"My daughter, I think you have found this thing for a reason."

He reached out and pushed the stone back into place.

Then he drew her to her feet, and led her out of the grove.

"The time has come."

Chapter Six

A truth by
the flame

"My daughter, I have been keeping a secret for many years. I did it to keep you safe. I hope you will forgive me."

The flame of the oil lamp flickered on Papa Eze's face. He looked unfamiliar and worn, like one of the carvings in his ancestor's shrine.

"Papa! There is nothing to forgive!"

Ada's heart was racing. She had never seen her father like this. It felt as if the world she knew was shifting around her and she was fearful of what would come next.

"I already know the truth…" she protested. "I know that you found me in the forest. Our ancestors differ – but I am still your daughter…"

He laughed.

"Of course you are. You will always be – and I will be your Papa, for as long as you want me to be."

Then he looked at her, and his kind eyes were touched with a deeper sadness.

"The time has come for you to know the full story. I did not tell you when you were younger because I thought it was the best way to protect you. But that has changed…"

He pulled his shawl around his shoulders.

"Today I went to see a man that I do not like. He is a diviner Ada. One who finds answers to our most difficult problems. But he is one that I do not trust."

"Why… so why did you go?"

Papa Eze shrugged.

"Sometimes we must seek for answers beyond ourselves. People think I am wise and it is true I am skilled in plant lore. They come to me for healing, and I help them if I can."

"Yes Papa."

"But recently… I have found that I could not

help myself, so I sought the advice of this man.

"He told me that he knows the cause of my pain. He said that I am being punished for keeping the truth from you..."

Eze laughed and shook his head. "Ujo is used to working out people's secrets I think. He is a cunning man, very crafty. And he seemed to guess a lot. But still...

"He gave me his advice. I was not convinced, but when I saw that you had found it, this thing, I made up my mind."

He unwrapped it again – the object from beneath the stone – and Ada gazed at it, now shining brightly in the light of the flame.

It was intricate and beautiful, a brass armlet decorated with carvings of warriors and leopards. Up close, each leopard's spot was shown as a delicately made hole.

"Daughter, there is a reason you found this treasure tonight – " he lifted her wrist, and he slid the armlet onto it " – it belongs to you. And now I must tell you why."

******

"The night you were born, your mother had to run for her life. She was wearing this very armlet. She left her home in the Edo city and fled into the rainforest."

"My mother lived in the forest?"

"Yes, because she was Edo," replied Papa Eze.

"But why... why did she leave?"

"Where many people live, there can also be danger," sighed Papa Eze. "Your mother was no ordinary woman. She was from a powerful family – the most powerful family. Ada, your mother was a wife to the Ogiso himself. You are the sky-king's daughter."

His eyes watched her intently in the flame light, and she stared back at him.

"The sky-king?"

"Yes my child. You are a princess of the royal house, as your mother was a queen."

Ada gasped.

"Her name was Akele," continued Papa Eze. "She was young and perhaps naïve. One night, word reached her that a powerful warrior – one trusted by the king – had accused her of bringing bad luck to the land. This chief said Akele was an evil omen. And he convinced your father, the Ogiso."

"Evil? But why would he say that?"

Papa Eze sighed and shook his head.

"A man may tell lies for many reasons. Sometimes it is jealousy. Sometimes spite. In this case, I believe the warrior chief had failed in battle and wanted to make an excuse – he needed to give the Ogiso a reason as to why he had failed. So, he blamed Akele.

"Luckily, your mother learned of his lie just in time. And she fled into the night, dashing out through the city gates. She was fearful of the dark and the wild trees beyond the city – but it was still safer than the certain death she had left behind. It was the rainy season, the ground was muddy and slippery. Poor Akele, I have often thought how she must have struggled."

"Were you there? How did you know her?" asked Ada.

"I wasn't there, child. I found Akele the next morning while I was looking for plants in the forest.

I heard somebody breathing heavily among the bushes, and when I looked I found her – covered in mud. And groaning."

Papa Eze turned away and sighed.

"When I knelt and touched her hand, her eyes opened. I told her to lie still. She was tearful and begged me to help.

"And I did. You were born, my child – you came crying into the world."

Papa Eze's eyes were full of joy, glistening with tears.

"Your mother's breathing was shallow, so I cradled you for her. She asked me to care for you and she pressed this precious armlet into my hands. 'When she grows, give her this.' 'Yes, yes,' I replied, all the time thinking that she would give it to you herself."

"What happened to her?" whispered Ada – although she dreaded the answer that she knew would come.

"Your mother died my child. I am sorry – " he stared into the flame for a moment before continuing.

"But this is not the end of the story. She cried out before she died – and it was then that I saw she had given birth to a second child. You had a brother. A twin."

He leaned forward to comfort Ada. Her eyes were running with tears now.

Papa continued:

"I tore a piece of cloth from your mother's wrapper – I hated to do it but I had to, to wrap you in. I sat with her for a long time, and I would have stayed longer, but then I heard voices approaching. Two men, carrying swords.

"Just in time, I hid. Your mother escaped her enemies, but only through death. Then I escaped too, with you."

He paused for a moment, adjusting the lamp.

"Each day it makes me sad that I could not also keep your brother safe," he said, holding her face in in his hands. "But I have done my best. And I have never revealed the truth – for words travel child. Stranger talks to stranger. And I did not want news of your survival to reach the Edo kingdom. We could not be found to be sheltering you – it would

57

have brought trouble to our village and death for you."

Ada looked at the bronze armlet on her wrist. She had never seen anything so beautiful but it was too big for her.

She pictured how her mother must have looked wearing it.

But then she slipped it off and passed it back to Papa Eze.

"We can put it back," she whispered. "You've told me the secret now Papa, so your pain will go."

Papa Eze took the armlet but said nothing.

****

The next day the sun rose in the east and climbed above the village as it always did, and life went on as normal. Families went to work on their land, some of the men set out to hunt, women sat at their looms weaving, children ran between homes, playing, or on errands and young Chika, in her home nearby, comforted her new baby.

Ada knotted her wrapper neatly about her body and tucked the end in tightly, the way Mama Ginika

58

had taught her. She was thinking how the sun must also be shining on the great Edo city, deep in the forest. It was no longer only a far off place from a fireside story. Suddenly it had become real to her.

She thought about her mother. And the twin brother she had lost.

And in the city – although Ada could not know it – at that moment, a man was thinking about her.

****

The man was kneeling.

He was in one of the maze of rooms, deep in the royal palace. Two mighty elephant tusks stood at either side of the doorway and a display of spears, knives and swords hung along the walls.

The man bowed again before the figure seated in front of him.

"Humble greetings, Chief Obiro."

"Who are you? Why do you disturb me? Speak."

"My name is Ujo, my chief. I am a diviner from the lands across the great river. I have come with news that may be of interest to you."

Ujo risked glancing up, meeting the war chief's

eyes – and he flinched at the hardness of the gaze looking back at him.

Chief Obiro was lean, his face scarred from battle. Ujo saw that he was wearing a necklace of leopard's teeth and his knotted arms spoke of hidden strength.

He was a famed leader of Edo armies, trusted by the Ogiso himself.

"Well?"

"I have travelled for days my lord. I am a humble man, a poor man…"

Chief Obiro smiled coldly.

"And you think that I will pay you?"

Ujo lowered his eyes again.

"My chief…"

For a moment, there was no sound except footsteps and the hushed conversation of two slaves passing outside the door.

Chief Obiro was turning a knife over in his hands, studying the blade.

"And how much do you think your information is worth?"

"Very much, my chief, I truly believe it. But…" Ujo glanced up again, risking everything now "…I would settle for three bags of cowrie shells."

Chief Obiro looked at him with contempt.

Beyond his shoulder, a window opened onto an enclosed courtyard garden, where a parrot paced along a branch, rubbing its beak.

And then Chief Obiro laughed.

"Three bags. Very well, they will be yours, if your information pleases me. If not you will leave here without one of your ears."

"My chief?"

"That is my bargain. Take it or not."

Ujo bowed – "I humbly thank you chief" – and the words spilled out of him. Words that told of the herbalist Eze, and the long hidden secret of the dead queen's child, Ada and her twin brother.

Chief Obiro listened. And learned.

And though his gaze remained fixed and unflinching, behind his eyes his thoughts were racing.

****

A short while later Ujo took his blood money, and left as quickly as he dared. The ruthless

Obiro would now send hunters to find the herbalist and his daughter, Ujo was sure of it – Obiro would want none of Queen Akele's children to survive. But that was no concern of his.

He slipped through the palace gates, bowing to the guards, and quickly lost himself in the crowded lanes.

He hurried along the street of iron-workers, past the workshops where weapon makers' fires burned bright, and where newly made tools were stacked against walls, ready for digging and clearing land.

He slipped past the quarter where the potters did their trade, and where – today – a skilled artist from the famous city of Ife was teaching her apprentices how to create portrait heads that captured not just the likeness of a person, but something of their spirit too; past the weaving sheds, the timber stores, the ancient musical instrument maker's shop and the hushed studio where ivory was being shaped and carved into delicate ornaments.

And he paid attention to none of it.

He had his cowries.

He just wanted out.

Chapter Seven

A warning
and a lie

A few days after she had found the secret armlet, Ada was sitting in the shade, repairing a worn mat with new threads of raffia. It was fiddly work, and all the more difficult because she was also watching Papa Eze.

She was worried about him.

Papa was with Mbe, showing him how to lay palm leaves out in the sun. When the leaves were dry, they would be stripped and used to make fibres for weaving. Mbe was nodding, his face as serious as ever.

But Ada could see that Papa was still moving stiffly. Had his pain not eased? Ujo had promised that if Papa revealed his secret, he would feel better…

Papa Eze had not spoken of it again, but Ada could tell that he was still troubled. She put down the mat. Mbe was already heading off, to fetch more bundles of palm. This would be a good time to take Papa some food.

But at that moment, as she stood, she spotted a familiar figure, hurrying towards them through the village.

Mama Ginika was striding purposefully, moving more quickly than Ada had ever seen before, her stick striking at the ground.

It made Ada feel uneasy.

****

Papa Eze turned to greet Mama Ginika warmly, but in a moment his body language changed. Ada couldn't hear what they were talking about, but Papa was leaning in, listening intently. After a while he glanced up at the path, the one that led towards the hill and Mama Ginika's home.

And then the old woman was holding both his hands in hers, and he was nodding.

Suddenly Papa was crossing the garden towards Ada.

"Daughter – hurry now. Run and fetch Mbe as fast as you can."

****

Ada ran to find Mbe, and when the two of them came back they found Mama Ginika waiting for them at the door. There was no sign of Papa Eze.

"Follow me children. And you – " she looked at Mbe. "Bring your spear young man."

"Where are we going?" he asked.

"Not far."

The old woman set off, walking ahead, and they followed, skirting the edge of the village.

"Where is Papa? What's happening?" asked Ada.

"Quiet now child! I am too old to walk and talk at the same time."

She led them out past the grazing cattle, through the long grass to the great baobab trees. Then she stopped at last to catch her breath.

"Your Papa will join us here soon. Now let's sit."

And as the old woman lowered herself to the ground and rested her back against one of the great trunks, she told them what had happened.

****

"I first heard the rumours yesterday, from a trader. I should have paid more attention, but I did not realise what it meant.

"This man – his name is Idris – he used to trade cloth with my husband. They did business together for many years. My husband is long dead, but whenever Idris is passing on the road, he still stops to see how I am and buy some of our best cloth. He is a good man, and he travels, far and wide.

"He visited yesterday and told me of a strange thing. There is a rumour that men from the Edo city have crossed the river into our lands. Warriors. They are going from village to village, asking questions." Mama Ginka looked directy at Ada. " – searching for a herbalist and a girl."

Ada gasped.

"Don't worry child, you are safe here. The spirits of these great trees will keep us hidden. I used

66

to play here when I was a child, and once they protected me from a leopard."

Mbe was staring at Mama Ginika.

"Why are Edo warriors looking for Ada?"

"Wait, let me finish. Today, just this afternoon, I discovered that the rumours were true. A group of men came along the road and stopped at my house. They said they want to find a man called Eze."

Ada put her hand to her mouth.

"Don't worry," the old lady shook her head. "They won't come yet. I didn't trust these men, child. I didn't like the look of them at all," she tutted. "Even in a different language, I can tell when people are lying to me, so I told them a small lie of my own. I said that Eze and his daughter had just gone away for a few days, gathering herbs. I told them to hurry after the morning sun, as you had not long left."

"Thank you Mama!"

"But you haven't explained!" demanded Mbe. "Why are they hunting for Papa Eze and Ada?"

"That is not our business to know," replied Mama Ginika. "Unless Ada wishes to tell us. We will wait here until Papa Eze comes. And then we will decide what to do."

Mama Ginika folded her arms and they sat in silence for a moment, with no sound but the wind in the grass and the birdsong in the branches above them – a pair of bushshrikes flitting back and forth, taking insects to their young.

"I will tell you what I know," said Ada after a while, looking at Mbe.

And, as the three of them waited for Papa, she told her story, finishing with:

"The Edo warrior chief wanted my mother dead."

Chapter Eight

Papa Eze's plan

The afternoon grew late. Still Papa Eze didn't appear.

Mama Ginika leaned against the tree. Her eyes were closed. But she was not asleep. Every so often Ada noticed her looking towards the village.

Until finally Papa came, stick in hand and bags slung across his back.

"Thank you for looking after these children, Mama."

"It is no trouble at all," she replied. "It is too long since I had a good reason to sit still like this."

Ada helped the old woman to her feet, and she stood leaning on her stick.

"Well Papa, have you decided what to do?" Mama Ginika asked.

"I have. Children, we must leave our home for a while."

"So you think these warriors are hunting for you?" frowned Mama Ginika.

"I fear so," he replied.

"But we don't have to run," protested Mbe, raising his spear. "We can fight them!"

But Papa Eze held up his hand.

"You are brave Mbe. And I know our neighbours will help, if we ask. But how many will be hurt? And if we win, will more Edo fighters come? Will we have a war?"

Mbe lowered his spear.

"A time to use your spear will come," said Papa. "But it is not now."

****

Mama Ginika stood watching, a lone figure beneath the trees, as they walked away. Papa Eze went ahead. Ada and Mbe followed. The moon was rising now, and the sounds of the savannah changed. The calls of birds were replaced by a chorus of insects, and the yap and scuffle of animals hunting out in the long grass.

After a while, Papa found a rock for them to sit against and said they should take turns to keep watch. He would stay awake first.

As Ada fell asleep, she tried to make sense of the day.

It seemed to her that she was no longer sure where home was. The village that she had grown up in was not the land of her ancestors.

Her ancestors were Edo. And now the Edo were hunting her.

****

Ada opened her eyes but the sun had not yet risen. Papa had got a fire going.

"Wake up children," he was saying softly.

Beside her, Mbe was sitting up yawning.

"This is for you. And this for you," Papa passed each of them one of the bags he'd brought from home.

"Food for three days. Supplies. Ada, your armlet is in here too, wrapped up safely. Keep it hidden until you reach your new home."

They looked at each other – what did he mean? – but then he held their hands in his.

"We must go separate ways for a while. The Edo warriors will soon find out that we left together. They will search for an old man travelling with two children. We must not be seen with each other."

"Do not worry Papa Eze," said Mbe. "I will die before I let any harm come to Ada."

Ada nodded – "Yes, we will be fine" – but she did not feel as brave and certain as she sounded and wondered if it was the same with Mbe.

Papa had been warming a pot over the fire. It now began to steam and he lifted it off with a stick. He divided the liquid into three carved bowls.

"Drink, both of you. It will give you strength."

Ada cupped the bowl and breathed in the sweet aroma.

"It is good," said Mbe.

And Papa explained.

"When it is light I want you to travel as fast as you can. You will be quicker without me. As soon as the sun rises, put it behind you and walk west. By the afternoon you will reach the great river."

He leaned forward with his stick, and by the firelight he scratched a line in the earth.

"When you reach the river – here – turn aside. Follow the flow of the water. Keep walking for a day then ask for a man named Chief Iwe."

He looked at them to make sure they had understood.

Mbe nodded solemnly.

"And will you be following us Papa?" asked Ada. "Shall we wait for you?"

"I will not be following. I have a different journey to make. But I will find you. We will meet again as soon as it is safe, I promise."

"But why Chief Iwe? Who is this man?"

Papa Eze stirred the fire. He collected the bowls together and packed them away. Then he looked at Ada.

"He is the one who sheltered your brother."

****

And by the firelight, Papa Eze told them how he had saved the Edo queen's newborn twins, but then been chased by the warrior chief's men.

73

He had stumbled through the trees and along
hidden paths, ever fearful of the warriors behind
him. His legs had cried out for rest but he had
ignored the pain and kept moving, carrying both
children, one in each aching arm.

And when he'd thought he could go no further,
he had found help. At the river's edge, a man was
sitting beside a canoe.

"Greetings friend. Where are you running to?"

As Papa had collapsed, the man rushed to help.

He shared his food and water. And while Papa
drank, the man had taken one of the infants and
cradled him.

"We must keep these children safe, and never
speak of this day," both had agreed.

The man knew of a village where the head man –
Chief Iwe – was always looking for help to work his
land. He was said to be happy to take in orphans, to
give them shelter. So there would surely be a place
for the infant boy there.

And before any watching eyes in the forest could
see them, each went his own way, each with a new
child to care for. One with the girl. The other with

the boy. Separating the twins was the best way to protect them.

Papa finished the story, then settled back to sleep.

"Rest now daughter," he said, as the fire flickered low. "Tomorrow you must travel fast. Go with my blessing and find your brother."

Chapter Nine

Heading north

The sun was just below the horizon when Ada woke again.

Beside her Mbe was stirring too. The fire had died to ashes.

And Papa was gone.

"Are you OK?" whispered Mbe.

She nodded, sitting up.

"Yes. You?"

"Yes."

Ada stood and turned her back to the spreading dawn.

And when, a moment later, the sun rose directly behind her, a new shadow sprang out from her feet and tumbled away across the grass.

"That way," she pointed, and her shadow pointed too.

Mbe gathered the bags.

"Let's race the sun to the river."

They set off. And, whether it was the drink Papa had given them or the clear words he had spoken, at that moment neither was afraid.

They avoided the herdsmen's trails. And they steered away from villages, whenever they caught glimpse of a thatched roof or a plume of smoke in the distance.

As the sun rose, the country opened before them, grassland dotted with trees and shrubs.

They passed a watering hole where a herd of thick-horned buffalo grazed, ears flicking against the irritation of flies.

"Be watchful," warned Ada. "Predators are drawn to such places."

"And the buffalo are not friendly!" replied Mbe.

Ada glanced at Mbe, and noticed how he walked tall and showed no fear.

He found her a long stick, almost as good as his spear. When they stopped to eat, he borrowed Ada's knife and sharpened the stick to a point for her.

They shared some fruit and after a short rest,

they went on.

Every so often Ada looked behind, to check that no-one was following.

****

Back at the village, Mama Ginika was sitting by her door weaving.

She had a good view down the hill.

She could see the young men, driving their cattle slowly across the valley.

Later, she saw a group of children and women sauntering towards the lake with bundles of cloth.

And around mid morning she spotted three tall figures passing along the crest of the hill.

Her eyes narrowed and she stood up for a better view.

The three men had fine curved swords slung at their sides and Mama Ginika recognised the shape of them at once: umozo swords, used by the Edo.

The men were moving very quickly, and soon they vanished from sight – out towards the ancient baobabs.

Mama Ginika forgot her loom, letting it tumble

to the floor. Inside her house, she knelt at her ancestor's shrine.

"Watch over those dear children. Keep them from harm!"

******

The children kept walking through the heat of the day.

At last, by the time the sun was setting, they reached the top of a bank and saw it – the curving line of the river, shimmering orange and gold in the setting sun.

They felt the light of it on their faces.

"Just like Papa said," grinned Mbe. "Now we turn and follow it."

"To the place where the reeds grow tall," smiled Ada – but an instant later the words froze on her lips.

From somewhere behind echoed a long, high note – a whistle. It was followed by three quick shrills in reply.

"What was that?" frowned Ada, turning.

"Down!" cried Mbe suddenly.

He dragged her away from the top of the bank and they scrambled together down the slope towards the river.

The vegetation grew denser, closing in behind them.

"It's the Edo!" exclaimed Mbe. "Come on!"

The ground began to feel soft and damp under foot, and a forest of tall reeds was growing up. They stumbled onto a narrow path, bending and curving through the vegetation.

"Don't stop…" urged Mbe from behind.

A moment later Ada saw, just visible above the rushes, the top of a thatched roof.

She ran towards it wildly, not caring where she trod. But Mbe turned aside

"Over here!" he hissed, ducking off the path.

They crouched down together in the reeds – only just in time. Moments later heavy footsteps pounded by, an arms-length away.

Then, before the children could move again, someone shouted. It was in a language they could not understand, but its meaning was clear.

The hunters had found them.

Chapter Ten

The great river

The thicket in front of Ada suddenly thrust open – she shrank back and Mbe scrambled to lift his spear – a man was facing them, knife in hand. He glared, gesturing for them to be silent – *don't make a sound!*

Then he spoke, his voice a low, urgent whisper.

"I've been watching you. Tell me why those men are following you."

"Sir, please help us," hissed Mbe.

"What do they want? What have you done?"

"They're going to hurt my sister!"

The man's eyes narrowed.

He looked at Ada, then back to Mbe.

"My name is Kene," he said, finally. "Wait here."

He slipped away into the long rushes, instantly vanishing.

The children waited. Ada grabbed Mbe's hand

and he held hers tightly.

Then they heard sounds again from the direction of the path.

****

K ene reappeared.

"Quickly. This way."

They were at the riverside now. And Kene was dragging something, scraping through the rushes – a long canoe – sliding it down into the dark water.

"Get in."

The thin boat rocked as the children climbed in, Ada first then Mbe. Kene stood knee-deep holding it steady. Then, with one easy movement, he climbed in too and sent the canoe gliding away from the bank.

"Lie down low and cover yourselves," he said, sweeping his paddle into the water.

And then they were moving fast, out into the wide river, the reeded banks on each side rushed past while the children lay with their faces pressed low, both praying for the evening shadows to hide them.

"What have you done? Why are those men hunting you?"

Kene had guided his canoe across the water and slipped beneath the overhanging trees there.

Through the branches, Ada could see the distant bank.

In the last of the light, she had the impression of figures moving about among the reeds.

"They came to our village. They're warriors from the Edo city," said Mbe.

"Our father said we must flee," added Ada.

"Why did the Edo come to your village? Who is your father?"

"He's herbalist, a good man," said Ada, ignoring the first question – and before Kene could ask again, she went on: "We are looking for the village where Chief Iwe lives. It is in the south, close to the rainforest. Papa said we will be safe there, and he will meet us."

"Chief Iwe…" Kene repeated.

After a pause, he nodded towards the high bank above them, where the trees were leaning out.

"Sleep up there tonight. Keep quiet and you

should be safe. I will return in the morning."

The children scrambled up.   In the tree top they stayed quiet, too frightened to make any noise.

Ada reached into her bag, feeling for the armlet again. But this time she heard no warning voice.

Then despite their fears, exhaustion took over and they fell asleep in the dense branches.

****

At first light Kene returned.
"I will take you to the place you are seeking," he said. "Or at least most of the way. It is a full morning down the river but I need to go that way anyway."

Mbe bowed his head.

"Thank you sir."

Ada bowed her head too.   "Do you know Chief Iwe?"

"I know a man of that name. Climb in quick and keep hidden," he replied. "Your hunters won't be far away and if they are true Edo warriors you will be lucky to escape. Lie very still."

They saw that he had put a bundle of matting in

his boat and they used it to cover themselves.

Kene laughed.

"Now you will both just vanish! Your enemies will believe you've been swallowed by the water…"

And twisting against the paddle, he thrust them forwards.

Ada lay looking up at the morning sky – clear and blue – and watched the riverside branches flitting above her. Then the branches were gone as the boat eased out into the river's deep currents, and there was only the sky and the birds.

Beside her Mbe breathed deeply and easily. The sound made Ada feel glad.

****

As the water carried them south, mile by mile, Kene told them stories about the lives of the fisher folk whose villages they passed, and whose men were out on the river too. And he pointed out two bigger boats – longer and wider than his own. These were traders from the north, guiding their boats down as far as the great forest.

"Many cowries change hands – the forest

kingdom is rich in its craftworks but hungry for
supplies. The Ogiso's men venture out far and wide
along the great rivers and across the land, to meet
with the traders and find cloth, metals, ivory and
many other things.

"The place you are going to is a trading village,
close to the forest. The man you seek – Chief Iwe
– is the head man. He has grown rich on trade."

But now Kene was looking at something else on
the riverbank.

"Be watchful. Treat them with respect," he said.

The children turned and followed his gaze. On
a muddy shore not far off, three huge crocodiles
basked, totally still, their mouths gaping.

"Are they dangerous?" asked Mbe.

"Of course. When their spirits are hungry. But
do not fear the crocodile you see in front of you –
fear the one who lies hidden. Yesterday you were
foolish rushing blindly to the river. You met me, but
you could have met him.

"You have nothing to fear, if you are respectful,"
he said. "And remember – in the forest kingdom,
the Ogiso himself is said by some to be like a

crocodile."

The children stared at each other, but Kene laughed.

"No, he does not have clawed feet! Even though he is descended from a god, he looks just like a man. But I hear that he can be unforgiving. And he has the power of life and death."

****

Finally, their journey ended.

Before Kene left them they sat for a while with the canoe drawn up on the bank, sharing their food.

"Children. I hope your Papa comes soon," he said. Then he added: "Chief Iwe is a great man but he is ruthless... be careful when you meet him."

"We will," nodded Mbe, respectfully.

Kene pointed towards the track that led up from the shore.

"You see this path? It has been trodden by many traders. You will not get lost."

They left then. As they climbed away from the river, he called out to them.

"In a few days I will pass this way again. You can return with me if you need to."

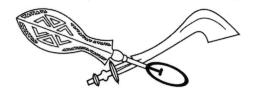

Part
Two

Chapter Eleven

Chief Iwe

Yesterday they had been desperate to reach the river. Now they had crossed it.

The path trailed over open grasslands dotted with trees, not so different from home. But still, both children felt as if they had strayed out of their own world and into a strange country.

Mbe glanced at Ada.

"Kene was a nice man. He reminded me of Papa Eze."

"Yes," answered Ada. "He was very kind. If he hadn't helped us those warriors would have caught us for sure."

Mbe shuddered and glanced back.

"They got too close."

"Do you think we are safe now?"

"We have come a long way," he replied. "And

thanks to Kene we left no trail to follow…"

Mbe pointed towards a thin plume of smoke rising in the distance. He frowned.

"We must remember what Kene said about Chief Iwe."

"Don't worry," said Ada. "If we need to, we can come back to the river."

She put her hand on his arm.

"Thank you Mbe."

"For what?"

"For putting your life in danger because of me."

He laughed, and shrugged.

"Oh no problem. I promised Papa."

But inside, he felt a glow of happiness.

****

The path grew wider, where it had been trampled by many feet and hooves. The smoke plume was rising directly ahead, and they could see buildings beyond a line of trees.

Mbe gestured to Ada.

"Quick, over here."

Beside the path an ancient, twisted tree was

growing hard up against a massive rock, almost as if it had emerged from beneath it.

Mbe knelt down.

"Let's hide our things here."

Ada nodded.

They emptied what was left of their food into one bag, and put everything else – including the precious ornament – into the other. This, they pressed against the base of the stone, and covered with rocks and earth. Mbe scattered grass across the top.

Then Ada had an idea of her own.

She grabbed up more of the earth in her hands and began rubbing it into the palms of her hands, and onto her knees.

"What are you doing?"

"Chief Iwe is not to be trusted. So let's disguise who we really are – let's just seem like poor children looking for food and rest."

They shuffled on, carrying one bag between them, now looking ragged and tired.

When they reached the line of trees, a man sauntered out and leaned on his spear.

He said nothing, but stood blocking their way.

The children stopped and Mbe bowed respectfully.

"Please sir, we are looking for Chief Iwe."

"What business do you have with him?"

"Our father sent us. He told us to ask Chief Iwe for help. We need food. We can work. I am a strong worker. So is my sister here."

The man shrugged.

"So you say. Chief Iwe will decide."

He gestured, with a flick of his eyes: *follow the path.*

****

They continued on, feeling themselves watched from behind – and also from the land beside the track, where people now stopped in their work to look at them.

The path led straight onto an impressive compound – and to the entrance in its red earth walls.

A woman stood there, with her hands on her hips, and it seemed to Ada almost as if she were waiting for them. She had similar look to the man they had just spoken too – a strong, proud face, but with eyes showing little kindness.

"You've come looking for food I suppose?"

"Yes, Ma. Thank you Ma – " Mbe gestured back towards the trees " – the man said we should speak to Chief Iwe."

"The man said that, eh? Well then, I suppose you'd best go in."

She pointed into the compound.

Within, Ada saw a wide, open space with groups of buildings of different sizes, mostly well kept, with new thatched roofs. The largest of these, with the highest roof, stood facing the gate.

"Over there," said the woman. "Wait until you are called."

****

They went where they were told, into one of the simpler houses a little way from the main building. Inside was a plain earth floor and no windows.

Two men sat on the floor in gloomy silence and

hardly seemed to notice when Ada and Mbe ducked in through the door. In the far corner was a young boy, knees drawn up to his chin. His eyes flashed suspiciously at Mbe, then looked away.

Ada sat on the floor too, leaning against the earth wall. Mbe sat beside her.

****

The morning passed. Through the doorway Ada caught glimpses of people at work around the compound, men carrying firewood, children running past on errands – the sounds of chatter, someone giving instructions, laughter and a shout – then, around noon, a large man looked in on them. He pointed at the men.

"You two."

They glanced sourly at each other – there was no love between them, Ada thought – then they followed the man out, one after the other.

"Do you think they going to see Chief Iwe?" whispered Ada.

Mbe nodded.

"I think so. Maybe there is an argument between

them…"

The silence settled for a moment, then suddenly the boy in the corner spoke.

"Those two men hate each other," he said. "They are fighting over money."

Mbe nodded.

"And they have come to ask Chief Iwe for his judgement?"

The boy shrugged.

"Yes. But Chief Iwe will have them both punished for arguing."

Ada looked at him – he was scrawny, with dark, serious eyes. He seemed half her age, but it was hard to tell – he might just be small.

"What about you? Why are you here?"

The boy looked down.

"Last night while I was serving Chief Iwe and the elders I broke a bowl."

"Will you be punished too?"

The boy nodded.

"They will beat me."

Ada looked at Mbe.

Then she reached into her bag. She pulled out

a bundle of roasted palm nuts that Papa Eze had given her.

"Are you hungry? Quickly," she whispered, "eat these before anyone comes."

The boy looked at her amazed – then he took the nuts and ate hungrily.

"Thank you!"

"My name is Ada," she smiled.

The boy whispered back, "I'm Madu."

Ada watched him as he ate.

"Madu," she whispered. "Do you know all the boys here? We are looking for someone, a boy the same age as me – and he looks like me too…"

But before she could say any more, the large man returned and beckoned for Madu to follow.

****

It was late in the afternoon before Ada and Mbe were finally led into Chief Iwe's obi.

In the few moments she was outside, Ada looked around the compound again for any sign of someone who might be her brother. But apart from a few men, she could only see women and younger children.

Chief Iwe's home was finely decorated, unlike any room that Ada had seen before – the walls were painted with patterns in white, yellow, red and black.

Chief Iwe himself sat sprawled on a wide stool. He was a man in his middle years, his hair showing signs of grey, his shoulders still strong but his stomach no longer lean – its wide spread a sure sign of his wealth.

Mbe knelt and bowed his head.

Ada did the same.

"Respectful greetings Chief Iwe," said Mbe. "My sister and I are hungry. We're looking for somewhere to rest and somewhere to work…"

He glanced at Ada as he said it.

Chief Iwe raised his hand, and the woman at his shoulder, who had been cooling him with a fan of bird feathers, became still.

Chief Iwe leaned forward.

"You and your sister, eh? You want to work?"

"Yes Chief Iwe. I am young and strong. I can do any job."

"I am sure. So why are you so poor then? Where

is your family? Why do you beg for my help?"

Mbe hesitated.

"Our village was attacked by raiders from the south. A war. We fled into the forest…"

"Hmmm…" Chief Iwe nodded. "I have heard such stories before."

He looked at Ada

"You. What work do you offer me?"

Ada looked back at him, holding her gaze steady.

"I can cook, Chief Iwe. My father was a skilled herbalist – " (she remembered Mbe's lie just in time) "…and my brother here learnt everything from our father. He knows almost as much of herb lore as an elder."

"Does he indeed!" Chief Iwe snorted.

His voice had lost none of its sneer – but all the same, something about Ada's coolness seemed to make him pause.

"Well we will see," he said.

He beckoned to one of the younger men, one of his sons.

"This girl and her brother will stay tonight. They may be useful."

******

Chief Iwe's son led Ada and Mbe out of the compound and along the valley. As he walked, he swung a heavy stick in his hand, flicking the tops of the grass stalks.

Soon they came to a huddle of smaller dwellings, where people were gathered around a fire. The chatter grew quieter as they passed.

He led them on, always flicking with his stick. They came to a house that was half collapsed against a tree.

"In there," the young man nodded. "You'll find food and water. Don't leave until we call for you."

Mbe bowed.

"Thank you, sir. We will wait."

The man pointed his stick at Mbe for a moment, then turned and headed back along the hillside. Mbe squeezed Ada's hand.

"We did it!" he whispered. "We're in!"

Ada leaned into the room, checking that it really was empty.

"Yes," she replied. "But I hope we don't have to stay long. This place feels dangerous."

As they settled down to sleep, Ada was thinking about Papa Eze. And wondering when she would see him again.

Chapter Twelve

A meeting in the dark

Ada woke in the deep night. Mbe was asleep.

But something had disturbed her – some sound or movement outside.

Her hand reached for the stick, the one that Mbe had found beneath the tree and placed between them before they slept.

Then she saw – or imagined – a dark shape crossing the bamboo screen at the entrance.

She leaned forward – not breathing – and nudged the screen just a crack, wide enough to peep out.

And a voice hissed.

"Ada. Is that you?"

A small figure was crouching in the moonlight.

"Madu?"

"Yes, it's me, Madu! They wouldn't let me talk to you before."

He shot a nervous look over his shoulder.

"I shouldn't be here."

"Are you OK? Did they hurt you?"

But he ignored the question.

"You asked about a boy…"

Ada's heart skipped.

"Yes Madu! You mustn't tell anyone, but I think he is my brother…"

Madu nodded.

"There is a boy. He looks like you Ada. His name is Nosa. I can take you to him."

****

Madu ran sure-footed, leading her past the nearest dwellings and the last smouldering embers of a fire, then downhill into the darkness beside the river.

They followed the path as it twisted downwards and at each turn Madu looked back to make sure she was still following.

Once, Madu stopped dead, listening, and gestured for her to keep still. Then he ran on again until they reached the shelter of a great tree.

"Nosa is in there Ada," he said, pointing. "Many workers sleep there – but Chief Iwe always leaves two of his sons to guard it."

Just ahead Ada could see the black outline of a ditch and bank, and the conical shapes of more thatched-roofs.

"Wait here," whispered Madu, and before Ada could reply he had gone.

****

Ada waited. The leaves stirred in the night air, and she was glad that she'd kept the stick in her hand.

It was not much of a weapon, but it was better than nothing.

She heard a hog grunting somewhere across the river. A splash of water. A snapping twig.

Then suddenly a face appeared out of the darkness.

A boy was standing right in front of her. The same height. The same face. The same eyes looking back.

"Nosa?"

"Yes. I am Nosa," he replied confidently. "Madu said you are asking for me. Why? Who are you?"

Ada stepped forward and held out her hand.

"Do you not know?"

The boy gave no answer for a moment. He looked at her, staring at her face.

"No."

But still, he kept staring at her as if a thought – a strange thought – was forming in his mind.

"What do you want?" he asked.

"My name is Ada. I am your sister."

Nosa stepped back.

"That's not true! My mother died when I was born."

"And mine did too."

She reached out.

"Show me your hand. Look – " she lifted her own hand, pressing it palm to palm with his. "Our fingers are the same…"

108

"But where did you come from? How are you here?"

"I will tell you."

She pulled his hand gently, drawing him to sit down with her beneath the tree.

"You do not belong in this place Nosa, you should not be here. Do you want me to tell you who you really are?"

He was still staring.

"Yes…" he replied at last, his voice almost a whisper. "Tell me then…"

******

They spoke together for a long while. Ada told Nosa about herself, about her journey with Mbe, about Papa Eze, and the truth she had learnt since the night she had found the precious armlet.

He listened quietly, only occasionally nodding his head very slightly.

Ada asked him about his life.

"There's not much to tell… I work for Chief Iwe. I have always worked for Chief Iwe, for as long as I can remember." Nosa shrugged. "Chief

Iwe is a harsh master. And his sons are worse."

"Brother, we will find a way out."

There was a stirring in the bushes behind them suddenly and Ada's hand tightened.

But it was Madu.

"It will be light soon," the young boy warned.

Not long after, when Ada got back, she found Mbe still sleeping soundly. She settled down beside him and waited. It would soon be dawn, and she couldn't wait to tell him her news.

******

And at that moment far away, at the edge of the rainforest, Papa Eze sat huddled under a shawl. A tangled path lay ahead of him. It was too dangerous to tread at night but as soon as it was light he would have to follow it.

Chapter Thirteen

The guests

Ada started awake with the sunlight streaming onto her face – and Amaka, Chief Iwe's first wife, leaning over her.

"Hurry up. You are not allowed to sleep so late."

Ada sat up.

"I… I'm sorry… where is Mbe?"

"The boy is working. The crops need tending. And you should be working now."

"Sorry, I did not sleep well…"

Ada took a gulp from the water jar.

"Follow me. There's no time to eat now. There's much to do."

Amaka started off up the hill and Ada hurried after her with fist clenched tight – and as soon as the woman was looking the other way, she sneaked a handful of bambara beans into her mouth.

Tomorrow would be a feast day.

Amaka pointed to the shade beside the compound wall, now crowded with people, all busy cooking, cleaning, cutting ingredients, and talking in low voices.

"Many guests will be arriving today. Important men. There will be no time for rest."

Ada was shown to a pile of yams and given a knife.

There was no room in the shade, so she knelt with her back to the sun and began peeling.

But as she worked, she kept glancing around for any sign of Mbe – she was desperate to tell him about Nosa.

****

Finally she saw him. The morning had become hot, making the trees across the valley shimmer. Ada had finally found a place in the shade, squeezing in beside a group of women, who now sat talking with their backs to her.

At that moment two figures came into the compound. First came an old man, thin-legged with

a stick in his hand – and following him was Mbe.
He was struggling with a large bundle of reeds on
his shoulder.

The thin man disappeared into a doorway on the
far side of Chief Iwe's obi.

Behind him, Mbe let his burden drop to the
ground.

He stood there for a moment rubbing his hands.
Then he followed the man inside, dragging the
bundle into the opening.

******

Later, Ada was sent with a group to wash clothes
at the river's edge. The cool water felt good
as she bent over the flat stone, kneading the cloth
with her fists. But her back and her arms were soon
aching.

Around mid-afternoon there was a buzz of
excitement as a procession appeared on the path
above them. They sat back and watched as a line of
travellers passed – guests arriving for tomorrow's
feast. In front sauntered a group of finely dressed
men followed by a line of warriors – straight-

backed, with swords and spears.

Ada had never seen such impressive people. Others came behind, with bundles on their shoulders or slung between them on poles.

At the back, some way behind, came a strange figure in a flowing, brightly coloured gown. His hand tapped lightly on a drum tucked under his arm. When he saw the women watching he pointed at them – then his skirts suddenly swirled as he spun on his heel, kicking up dust, beating a sudden rhythm on the drum.

A moment later he was gone, leaving the women chatting excitedly about the coming feast.

The sun was low by the time the washing was done. Ada followed the others back up the hillside.

At a turn in the path, a sudden impulse took hold of her. She sat down in the long grass. Then she lay. None of the others seemed to notice, and the sound of their chatter grew more distant.

Ada kept still, feeling her heart beat. She thought about her home and about Papa Eze and, as she stared up to the sky, the dusk slowly deepened.

Hunger gnawed at her stomach and she felt

weak from lack of sleep. She wanted to eat – surely they would be eating soon? – but really, more than anything, she just wanted to be gone from this place.

And then, for some reason, a picture of Mama Ginika came to her mind. She saw the old woman standing over her, fists on her hips and shaking her head – 'Dear me! Why are you lying there, young lady? Don't you have important things to do?'

The sudden thought made Ada smile.

"Sorry Mama…" she whispered.

"Good girl. Get along then."

And Ada lifted herself and checked that nobody was watching.

She picked her way through the shadows, back towards the dwelling beneath the tree.

She ducked inside and pulled the screen closed. Then she waited, hoping that Mbe would soon come.

******

"Ada! I've brought you some food."
A hand was shaking her awake.

In the half darkness she felt a bowl being pressed into her hands.

"I can't stay long," Mbe whispered. "I shouldn't be here. I'm supposed to sleep in the compound now. And I don't know when we'll be able to talk again."

Ada sat, hungrily scooping the food into her mouth.

"I have news," she said. "I've found Nosa."

And she told him everything that had happened – about how Madu had come the previous night and taken her to her brother.

"It *is* him, Mbe, I know it. And he wants to leave with us."

"Thank the gods!" said Mbe. "I do not like this place Ada. The sooner we can leave, the better."

"Yes. So let's go back to the river – Kene will find us there. Then maybe we can stay with him until it's safe to go home to Papa."

Mbe glanced over his shoulder to the doorway.

"OK, but listen – I went out gathering wood today. We walked a long way and Chief Iwe's people are everywhere, even outside the valley."

Ada frowned.

"Do you think they'd try to stop us leaving?"

"Yes. We offered ourselves to Chief Iwe – now they'll say we belong to him."

They sat in silence for a moment, listening to the night sounds outside.

"We'll be careful then," Ada whispered. "Tomorrow night Mbe, everyone will be at the feast – we'll escape then."

He still looked anxious, and Ada squeezed his hand.

"Don't worry, we're a team. We just have to get through one more day."

"Yes," he said. "One more day."

Chapter Fourteen

The feast

The next morning Ada got to Chief Iwe's compound while it was still dark and sat under a tree, ready to work. Dawn brightened the eastern horizon. Two women swept the compound with brushes, but neither seemed to notice her.

Then more people began to gather. Amaka arrived with the sun, speaking sharply, giving out instructions – and Ada pressed herself to the back of the group. Today, all she wanted was to find Madu, get the message to Nosa and not be noticed.

"You. Where did you go last night?"

Amaka was in front of her, pointing.

"Nowhere," said Ada, keeping her eyes to the ground. "I went back to my dwelling. Where you told me."

"That is not *your* dwelling. And today, you do not

leave until I tell you."

Amaka squeezed her shoulder roughly.

"Do not think I am stupid."

Ada stared at the ground.

Her heart was beating fast as she joined
the others, sweeping their brooms around the
compound. The fire had been lit and the morning
meal was being prepared for Chief Iwe and his
guests.

****

A round midday Chief Iwe's seat was carried out
and set up in front of his obi, opposite the
compound entrance, with an awning of bright cloth
stretched over it to give shade.

Then the chief himself appeared, richly
dressed in blue and red, followed by his elder sons
and wives. He sat stern-faced to watch over the
preparations, cooled by the fan of feathers.

Through the long afternoon more guests arrived
and Chief Iwe waited to greet them. For some,
he stood, laughing and embracing them with his
strong arms. For others, the poorer farmers from

neighbouring lands, he stayed seated and waited for gifts to be laid at his feet before nodding and bidding them to come forward.

The warriors that Ada had seen the previous day were warmly and respectfully welcomed. They politely presented Chief Iwe with a bowl of kola nuts, but it was Chief Iwe who was keen to impress. He sprang to his feet and smiled as they approached.

"Welcome to my home – please, come and feast with us."

Ada was relieved to be sent out of the compound again. Lodgings were being prepared for guests.

"The feast will go on late," said Itohan, a thin woman who was showing her how to arrange the bedding. "Tomorrow Amaka will have us working again early."

Ada nodded. But she was thinking, tomorrow I will be gone.

As the others chatted she kept looking out for Madu.

****

Her chance came as she was following Itohan and the others back to the compound. A huddle of workers were coming towards them, carrying food for the guests.

Ada caught sight of Madu among them.

This might be her only chance.

As the two groups passed, Ada let the cloth that she was carrying fall to the ground. She walked on, pretending not to realise.

"Pay attention!" snapped the man leading Madu's group, pointing.

Ada turned, looking confused, and dropped another bundle of cloth.

Madu, whether he somehow understood or was just being kind, sprinted out before anyone could stop him to pick it up.

"Here," he said, handing it back to Ada.

"Thank you," – then under her breath – "tonight – can you bring Nosa again – ?"

Madu was already turning to go, and he said nothing.

But his eyes replied: *I will try.*

****

The drummer with the bright gown began a low beat late in the afternoon. Sitting in front of Chief Iwe's chair his fingers tapped out a steady rhythm that merged at first with the sounds of the day. But almost unnoticed the beat grew stronger and people stopped what they were doing to watch and listen and sway with the drum.

At that moment, as the sun began its final descent across the far side of the valley, it seemed to Ada that even here – even in this village, ruled over by Chief Iwe – there was a magic and a wonder in the world.

The faces of the people around her were bright and beautiful in the evening light, and with the smell of the cooking meat and wood smoke promising the feast to come; whatever worries and troubles they felt during the day, for tonight at least did not matter.

Ada felt a hand on her shoulder
Amaka.
"There is someone who wants to speak to you."
She was nodding towards the edge of the crowd.
There, she now noticed a group of tall figures,

standing apart from the feast – three warriors, and an older man.

The older man carried no weapon, but he stood proudly and he had the strong arms of someone used to work. He had greying hair and keen, watchful eyes.

"Come," Amaka ordered. "And mind your tongue. These are important guests from the forest kingdom."

Ada's mouth was suddenly dry. As she followed Amaka her heart was pounding.

These were the same warriors she had seen arriving yesterday, but only now did it occur to her that they might serve Chief Obiro – the very men sent to hunt her and Papa down.

How could she have been so careless?

One of the warriors had stepped forward and was smiling down at her.

He was tall, with a strong face. His hand was resting on the curve-bladed sword at his belt, his fingers lightly gripping the handle. The finely worked ornaments on his arms reminded Ada of her own precious armlet, now hidden under the rock beside the road.

"Where are you from?" asked the warrior, smiling. His voice was soft, heavily accented.

Ada bowed her head respectfully, but her mind went blank.

"My parents died," she stammered.

"Died? In the Edo city?"

"No, not there – we are farmers – from the north…"

The warrior nodded.

He looked intently at her face.

And then he spoke in Edo – a language that was strange to Ada – strange, and yet somehow she could tell the meaning.

He was saying that she looked very much like someone he had once known… an Edo woman…

Ada looked down, shaking her head.

"No, I am from the north," she repeated.

The warrior turned to his companions. They all looked to the older man. He said something – more words that Ada did not recognise – then shrugged.

"You may go," said the tall warrior, stepping back.

****

As soon as she was sure that Amaka was busy, Ada got out.

She walked through the compound gate, then ran for her life.

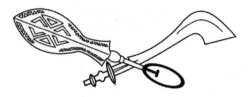

Part
Three

Chapter Fifteen

Escape!

The moon was a thin smile, low in the sky. Only a faint grey showed the line of the river. Ada ran straight towards it.

She had agreed to meet Mbe by the big rock. Maybe he was there already?

As she ran, the beat of the drum grew louder, seeming to chase at her heels.

Then she came to the curve in the track, and the twisted tree beside the rock loomed out of the darkness ahead.

And at that moment she heard a stir in the grass behind her, footsteps approaching fast.

"Mbe is that you?"

"Yes!"

"Thank goodness!"

They ducked down into the long grass.

Mbe sounded frightened.

"Did anyone see you leave?" he whispered.

"I don't think so... And I spoke to Madu. We couldn't talk much but I asked him to bring my brother. I think he understood."

"Let's be quick and find our things then."

He was searching around in the darkness at the base of the rock.

"Here Ada – "

She felt him press a bundle of cloth into her hands: the bag, with her mother's armlet still wrapped inside.

"Thank you."

The feel of the metal made her glad, and she slipped it over her wrist.

There was no point in hiding now. She would wear this precious thing tonight, just as her mother had done. She would make her ancestors proud.

Mbe was standing again, looking out across the hillside.

"Come," whispered Ada, standing beside him.

And she led the way through the darkness – towards the place where she hoped Madu would meet them.

****

"Ada!"

Madu was waiting beside the great tree. The instant he saw Ada, he ran to hug her.

"Well done Madu! And where is Nosa? Did you tell him?"

But the boy was staring up at her, eyes wide.

"Your brother has been tied up! They're going to punish him!"

"What? How do you mean?" Mbe crouched, his hands on the boy's shoulders. "Tell us! What's happened?"

"Chief Iwe's son – Uche he's called – started beating Nosa. He's always doing it! And for no reason. This time Nosa fought back! But then more came – and they tied Nosa up – and…" Madu stared at them. " – tomorrow they will take him in front of Chief Iwe…"

Ada pictured her brother held prisoner. And she was suddenly aware of the distant drums – a more urgent rhythm was rising up.

Voices were singing with the beat, wave after wave. It was the sound of the storm in the tree tops, the wind through the grass, the roar of the leopard, the thunder of hoofs, the fight for life.

Somewhere close by she knew Nosa was hearing the same sound. And his own heart must be full of dread.

"Ada – "

Mbe was talking to her again.

" – we can't wait any longer – "

She turned to Madu.

"Where is Nosa now? Can you take us to him?"

****

Madu darted along the path, ducking low past the small crowded homes where the farm workers slept – and they came to a place further on, where the ground had been cleared.

"There!" hissed Madu.

Ada could see a cage made with heavy wooden posts set close together – too close for even a child to squeeze through – and inside it, a crumpled shape, curled up on the ground.

"Keep down," hissed Mbe.

And at that moment a figure stepped out from

bushes and stood looking up at the sky – a boy not much older than Mbe, but old enough to be taller and stronger. He was standing guard, spear in hand.

"Uche," whispered Madu.

"The one who beat Nosa?"

"Yes."

Mbe reached for something at his belt. And a blade flashed in his hand.

"I kept this from my work today…"

For a moment they all looked at each other – and the knife.

None of them spoke.

Mbe turned the knife over in his hand.

"We've got to get Nosa out – " he whispered – at which Uche turned in their direction, seeming suddenly to hear.

In that instant Ada made up her mind.

"Stay here."

And she stepped out into the open ground – and headed straight towards the cage, her brother, and his captor.

****

132

The lie came easily to her. Fear made it seem real.

She held her hand against her side, imagining a pain, almost feeling it.

"Help us…" she gasped. She stumbled, reaching out for the young man, falling down in front of him.

Uche stepped back, raising his spear.

"There is fighting… " Ada panted. "…Chief Iwe was attacked… needs your help… "

Uche gasped – but his eyes were searching past her, looking for signs of a trick.

In desperation Ada raised her arm, showing her brass armlet.

"Chief Iwe gave me this – he was giving us all gifts and then the men attacked – please… " she broke off, sobbing.

And whether it was her tears, or the sight of the rich ornament, suddenly Uche was convinced.

"Keep watch here," he ordered – and sprinted into the darkness.

****

How long would they have? If enough time, only just.

Iwe's son would soon realise his mistake – maybe before he even reached the feast.

Then fear of his father would drive him back here. And his fear would be surely be matched by anger.

"Hurry!"

Mbe's stolen knife made quick work of the ropes and he dragged open the cage door.

Nosa scrambled to his knees, holding out his bound wrists.

"Sister?" he asked.

"Yes brother – we are here for you."

His face was bruised, his eye looked swollen and painful even in this darkness.

Mbe's knife cut through the bindings – hands first, then feet – and he leaned down to help Nosa stand.

"Hurry!" urged Madu again, so tense that he was almost hopping from foot to foot.

"Let's go," said Ada.

They left the cage hanging open and followed Madu into the night.

Chapter Sixteen

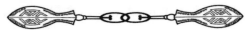

The hunted
and the hunters

The hunt began while it was still dark. By the time dawn was brightening the eastern sky, the children had run and stumbled a long way. In the distance, the calls and shouts of Chief Iwe's men had faded.

So at first it seemed they would escape.

They passed beyond the edge of the valley and followed the stars eastward, trying to find their way back to the river.

Time and again they stumbled in the darkness. Mbe went in front, beating and testing the way with his stick. As it grew light, the borders of the rainforest appeared ahead like a soft green line.

"Come on," urged Mbe.

If they could only reach it – at least they might find a place to hide.

But they were all tired, especially Madu, and Nosa's limp was getting worse.

****

"It's not much further," called Mbe, leading the way again.

But suddenly Madu cried out – "Uche!" – and looking behind Ada saw, sure enough, there was Iwe's son, close behind them. Eyes blazing, he was leading others with him, along the trail straight towards them. They were all carrying spears and knives.

Not far ahead, the bushes grew taller, and closer together, as if the rainforest were now reaching out with protective arms.

There was just a final, short run of open grass to cross.

"Nearly there! Come *on*!"

Mbe began to run, setting the pace, and Madu followed. Somehow even Nosa found some hidden reserve of endurance and forced himself to keep up. Ada had her arm around him, pulling him on.

They crashed together into the foliage – and into Mbe and Madu, who were standing dead still.

Facing him were the four Edo men from the feast.

****

I n a moment the Edo warriors had surrounded them, swords held to their faces.

The stick was pulled from Mbe's hand and dropped at his feet.

"You have put us to much trouble," one of them smiled. "Much trouble…"

His thickly accented words were spoken carefully. Ada recognised him as the tall man who had questioned her at the feast.

"Leave us alone!" cried Madu – but the warrior flashed a warning with his eyes – *be silent!*

"So, where do you young ones go in such hurry?" he continued, still smiling. "Not into Edo lands?"

"We just want to get away from Chief Iwe," pleaded Mbe.

"Ah yes, Chief Iwe," the warrior replied. "He

is not so happy today. I have never seen a man so vexed…"

He glanced back at his companions and they laughed.

Madu protested again – but this time Ada couldn't understand him. Whatever the boy was saying, it must be in the Edo tongue because the warrior grew serious and looked at him.

The older man, who had been watching, stepped forwards now. And to Ada's horror she saw that his dark eyes were staring at her armlet.

He said something – his voice quiet and commanding – and then the tall warrior was staring at her too.

"Where did you steal this thing from?"

He pointed to her wrist.

But before she could answer, Uche and his followers burst into the clearing.

The older man gave an instruction and the tall warrior raised his arm.

"Stop!"

Uche stopped, his spear half raised.

"Before you take these runaways, my companion

wishes to speak with them."

Uche hesitated, teeth bared, fist tensed on the handle of his weapon.

But then he shrugged.

"Very well. As our guests. But be quick…"

At his back, a murmur rose from his followers.

The tall Edo warrior nodded to his men and then the children were pushed at sword point further into the clearing. Now Ada watched as the older man leaned over Madu. He stared intently at the boy with his dark eyes, speaking words too softly to be heard.

When Madu turned towards her again, his eyes were wide.

"Ada," he said. "This man wants to know the name of your father."

Chapter Seventeen

The hidden paths

Ada felt her blood run cold and her voice die in her throat.

"Ada! He says you must answer quickly," hissed Madu.

But the man pushed the boy aside and spoke for himself.

"You are the herbalist's child. Do not lie."

Before Ada could find any words, her face had given her away.

The man nodded.

"And this –" he gestured towards Nosa. "He is your brother?"

"Please, he has done nothing wrong – " she heard herself saying.

But the Edo man raised his hand.

"Quiet, child."

He turned and spoke to the tall warrior – who

crossed the clearing to stand in front of Uche.

"Tell Chief Iwe that we will take these children to Edo city."

Ada felt her arm being pulled – she was being led away, into the forest.

"No!" Uche said. "They are ours. They belong to my family!"

Around them, as if in protest, the forest birds shrilled back.

The warrior raised his sword in front of him. Uche's gang crowded forward.

The last thing Ada saw, before the leaves swallowed the view, was the tall warrior blocking the way, his arms raised.

"These are the Ogiso's children. And this is his land. Leave now! Or feel his anger."

****

"Quickly now," said the older man. "Follow my men. Do not be frightened, we will not harm you."

Confused, Ada stumbled along the path after the warriors. The forest grew dense around them. And above them the sky was blocked out by layer upon layer of green, rising to a barely visible canopy. Sometimes, she caught sight of the briefest flash of blue sky, but it was impossibly high above them and immediately blocked out again.

And everywhere she looked was teeming with life. The forest air pressed around her, warm and damp – and alive with the buzz and flutter of darting wings.

Nosa stumbled in front of Ada, the tall warrior now followed at her back.

The sandy path forked. They took the smaller way, scrambling down into a gully. The trail was lost for a while as they ran through water, ankle deep, and the vegetation rose thick around them.

****

Finally, they were allowed to rest.

The children collapsed together beside the path. The tangle of undergrowth had been cut back, and the ground carefully trodden to make a small, open space.

But there was barely a glimpse of sky through

the branches above, and Ada noticed that the vines and creepers were already pressing in on every side. Whoever had cleared this space would need to do it again very soon.

The old man and the tall warrior had disappeared, and the other warriors sat apart, seeming to pay them no attention.

"Nosa – are you OK?" Ada whispered.

He looked up and nodded. His bruised eye was swollen shut.

"I am tired, sister. But this is the best day of my life – wherever we are going, nothing can be worse than Chief Iwe's place."

Madu sat beside Nosa, his thin arms wrapped protectively around the older boy – but his head had already nodded and he was fast asleep.

Nosa turned to Mbe.

"Thank you for helping us brother. I can never repay you."

"Brother, you will never have to."

****

How long they rested there, Ada had no way of knowing. In this dim light there were no shadows to reveal the time of day.

She fell asleep and when she woke she saw that the older man had returned with the tall warrior. They were sitting with the other two men, eating.

The tall warrior noticed Ada.

"Chief Iwe's people have not crossed our borders," he said, between mouthfuls. "They are afraid. But even so, they might follow us yet – they claimed that Chief Iwe himself would be coming, with lots of men."

"So we must go deeper in," said the older man man. "But first – come. Come eat."

Mbe, Madu and Nosa were sitting up.

"Here," said the man, beckoning them forwards. "Do not be afraid."

But Ada did not move – instead, she heard herself speak.

"Who are you?" she asked. "Are you Chief Obiro?"

And above them a parrot shrieked in protest as the man suddenly threw back his head and laughed.

Chapter Eighteen

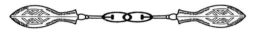

The shrine of Ogun

His name was Amenze.

The tall warrior was smiling too.

"Amenze is one of our great craftsman, famous in the Edo city," he said. "Chief Obiro is another great man in our city, but he is not our friend."

Then he looked at the children.

"We must be careful. Eat quickly, then we will go on and I will explain."

****

The two other warriors hung back – hiding among the trees with their bows and arrows, to make sure that no one was following – while everyone else set off again with Amenze along the path, this time walking not running.

Amenze spoke to them, haltingly, searching for the right words.

"What do you know of our city?"

"It is huge," said Madu. "Hundreds of people live there!"

Amenze laughed.

"Many more than that," and he lifted his arm towards the canopy above them. "Imagine a person for every leaf you see."

"Wow!" exclaimed Madu. "What do they all eat?"

"You will see for yourself soon enough. In the heart of this great forest, hidden from enemies, our Ogiso has had lands cleared for growing crops. Many people work the land – we do not lack for food."

"Do *you* farm there too?"

"Me? No! My trade is with metal…"

"Amenze is head of the iron workers' guild," said the tall warrior gently.

And when Madu looked at him blankly, Amenze explained.

"There is a guild in our city for every craft –

each guild is a great family. Each has its special knowledge and skills – and the secrets of its trade are passed down from father to son. We work for the Ogiso, and the Ogiso keeps us safe, and everything in order."

"What is the Ogiso like?" whispered Mbe.

"Ah," replied Amenze, "Our great king of the sky. He is as near to a god as it is possible to be on this earth. And powerful. We respect our Ogiso for though he is stern he keeps us safe. And our enemies fear him…"

And then he turned to Nosa and Ada.

"You know why Chief Obiro has been hunting for you, I take it?"

Ada replied and recounted everything that she knew – about how Papa Eze had found her and Nosa as babies – about how their mother had died.

Nosa listened, hearing the story again.

He looked at Amenze.

"I did not know any of this until my sister found me – and rescued me."

Amenze nodded.

"You have lived your life as a slave Nosa," he

147

said. "But you are the son of the king."

Nosa looked back at him.

"But what does this mean? For my sister and me?"

"It means you must be careful. You have powerful enemies."

Amenze suddenly stopped and turned aside from the path.

The children followed him into a clearing, barely wide enough for them to stand in. It was neatly kept though, with the ground clear of growth.

A large rock stood at the far side, and there was an iron rod in the middle of the clearing and a metal-tipped short spear.

Amenze and the tall warrior knelt in front of it. The children watched – sensing a watchfulness in the hushed air around them – as Amenze reached into his bag and scattered some kola nuts.

"Children," he whispered. "This is a shrine of Ogun, who is worshipped by warriors and metal workers. I have thanked him for bringing us together."

Then Amenze explained.

"We metal workers have always been great travellers. We venture far and share our skills with others of our trade. But we always stop at that shrine before we leave the forest – or when we come back – to ask for Ogun's protection."

"Is that why you were at Chief Iwe's compound?" asked Nosa.

"Yes. Chief Iwe can be useful. Your father, the Ogiso, controls the trade with him; Iwe is useful for the metals and ores that we need in our work. And he pays tribute to the Ogiso."

Then he looked at Ada.

"But this time, I believe mighty Ogun also had a purpose of his own. He led me to find you."

He stopped and lowered his voice.

"A few weeks ago, we began to hear reports – Chief Obiro was sending armed men out, hunting for some children."

"The men who came to our village," said Mbe.

"Yes," nodded Amenze. "We guildsmen learned of this. We have our spies too."

He looked at Ada.

"Remember when I spoke to you at Chief Iwe's

feast? I had a faint hope in my heart that you might be Queen Akele's daughter – you reminded me so much of her."

"If only I'd told you the truth then!" exclaimed Ada.

"You were right to be wary," he replied. "You did not know me. And anyway, Ogun brought us together again soon enough. When I next saw you, at the forest edge, I knew for sure who you were."

"How?"

"Ah, that is the most remarkable thing of all – "

But before he could answer, there was a call from the path ahead. It was the tall warrior.

"We should go now. It will soon be night."

Amenze turned to the children. "Chief Osawe is right. He is a great warrior and a great friend. We will go on now and finish our story later. We must reach safe shelter before the leopard awakes."

****

They hurried on in silence now, walking, running, and the forest light began to fade. The air shifted, the sounds of the birds and animals changed, and the trees with their dense, shiny leaves seemed to take on a new life. The slow moving chameleons, and the darting lizards, were now hard to spot. The bright feathered birds no longer swooped and flitted across their path.

Madu held Ada's hand. Where the path was wide enough Mbe walked beside Nosa, helping him on.

At last, Ada was relieved to see firelight dancing through the trees ahead.

Chapter Nineteen

A resting place

They stopped outside the clearing.

"Is this the city?" whispered Madu, peering to get a better view.

"No," laughed the tall warrior. "This is just a small place used by our people for travellers to rest. Wait here. I will go ahead and find us food and shelter."

When he had gone, Amenze gathered the children around him.

"You can stay here safe for a few days." He gestured to the tall warrior – "Chief Osawe here will watch over you while I go on to the city and make arrangements. I must speak to the guildsmen. I will be gone for a few days. You rest and regain your strength. And learn what you can of our Edo language."

"I speak it already."

"I know Madu – so you can teach the others. When we reach the city, we will all need to speak Edo. Especially Nosa and Ada, for they may meet the sky-king, their father."

Madu nodded solemnly.

"I will be a good teacher."

Ada glanced at Nosa. It had not occurred to her, until now, that this is where their journey might take them – to the Ogiso himself. Ever since leaving home her only thought had been to escape from danger and find Papa Eze again. She had never dreamt that her path might lead her this way, towards the very heart of the Edo kingdom – towards the sky-king himself.

Nosa seemed untroubled. Despite his exhaustion he was holding his head up.

"I will learn Edo," he said.

"Remember," said Amenze, "while you are here, be careful. Chief Obiro's men may stop here too, so do not tell anyone who you really are."

"We'll be careful."

Now Chief Osawe returned.

"Come. I have found a good place for us to stay."

******

A deep, impenetrable blackness settled through the rainforest and the Edo people drew into their round houses, shutting out the night.

In their travellers' shelter at the edge of the clearing, Chief Osawe fastened the screen across the doorway. In the distance they could hear the splash of a river, though no boats travelled on it during the night. Ada rememberd Kene's warnings about crocodiles.

Then, before they all settled down to sleep, Amenze finished his story.

"Ada, you asked how I was sure who you were when we met again at the forest border. I will tell you."

He pointed to her wrist – to the armlet.

"As soon as I saw this precious thing, I was certain. I have seen it before, you see, many years ago. When I was an apprentice, I helped my own master to make it. It was gift for your mother, Queen Akele."

Ada looked at him in wonder.

"You made this?"

"Yes – at least I helped to. And I believe its return to the city now is a sign. Maybe it was sent by Ogun himself! When your father sees what a fine daughter he has – and what a fine son – he will recognise the truth. And Chief Obiro will be punished."

Chapter Twenty

Speaking Edo

At first it was strange living in the rainforest. The children stayed close to their lodgings. They kept to themselves, sitting quietly at the edge of the clearing, watching tradesmen and travellers come and go on their way to and from the Edo city.

On the first night Ada had lain awake for a long while, worrying that Chief Iwe and his men were creeping in from the border with their knives, coming silently through the trees – but when she had finally fallen asleep, she'd dreamed that the forest paths began to twist around Chief Iwe, doubling back on him until he became lost. And all the while Chief Osawe and his warriors were watching from the trees, ready with their spears.

The next night Chief Iwe did not return to her

dreams – or any night after that.

They rested and Nosa's injuries continued to heal.

Madu helped Ada with the food. There seemed to be no shortage here – yams, beans, okra. And a new fruit that they had not seen before, but so sweet that the children delighted in stripping its tough skin from the long cane and chewing it greedily to get at its juice. Chief Osawe told them it was called okwere.

The small village in a vast sea of green began to feel like a sort of home. Or at least, in its own way, it felt safe.

In the evenings, Chief Osawe sat with them, telling them stories and playing akhue, a skillful game of spinning and knocking down seeds. Madu soon became obsessed by it.

And all the time now they spoke in Edo.

Gradually, like the forest itself, the Edo language began to seep into Ada's mind – and without noticing she began to speak and think in new words.

****

A few days later Amenze returned.

He sat down gratefully, resting his legs. And setting aside his bag he accepted the cocoyam porridge that Ada and Madu had been preparing together.

"My friends," he smiled. "Has young Madu been a good teacher? Can you all speak in the Edo tongue now?".

"Yes, I understand you now Amenze," replied Ada.

"I too," said Nosa. "I am ready to meet the king, our father."

Amenze nodded.

"That is good Nosa, for it is the plan I have made. Tomorrow we will go on to the city. And when we arrive, the guildsmen will meet you in secret, and speak with you both. After that… if all goes well, we will enter the palace."

Chapter Twenty One

The Edo city

The journey to the heart of the rainforest took them another three days. On the third morning, the path twisted along beside a river, and they began to see men fishing from canoes beneath the overhanging trees – small craft like the one Kene had rescued them in – and larger boats too, being paddled and steered along on the current.

Across the river the path joined a wider trail. Then another.

And suddenly the forest ended.

A great trench – large beyond imagining – had been dug out of the ground with a bank rising up behind it. This earthwork stretched away into the distance on either side, as if a giant had scored a deep line in the earth and scratched away all the tangled vegetation.

On one side of the line was the rainforest. On the other side was another world.

The great Edo city.

Ada would never forget her first sight of it.

The city was so bright in the sun! The sky opened wide and clear above her for the first time in days. And beyond the long trench stretched an open landscape of cultivated lands: neatly tended crop gardens with homes dotted among them beneath well kept groves of fruit trees and palms.

Further off in the distance, the city itself could be seen, where the buildings were larger and arranged more closely together. Even from here Ada could see that their thatched roofs were well maintained, and the walls beneath them freshly finished in reds and ochres. Above many of the larger buildings, trees waved in the gentle breeze, casting shade over hidden courtyard gardens beneath.

There were people everywhere – working in the land, talking together in groups, carrying goods into and out of the city along a network of paths. A line of warriors was jogging towards the trench, fully armed with swords and spears.

"See that wide road straight ahead? It leads to the great palace," said Amenze softly. "But we will take a different way, for now."

Chief Osawe was raising his hand in greeting towards the guards beside the earth bank, and they nodded back.

Amenze led the children onto a path that widened into a narrow lane.

Ada marvelled – its surface was smooth beneath her feet, pressed with fragments of pottery. And as they came into the city itself, she saw that the red clay walls of the buildings on either side were polished smooth.

"You will stay here, at my home," said Amenze and he ushered the children into a large compound with many thatched houses.

He gestured to a small empty building.

"Wait here and rest," he said. "My family will bring you food, but nobody will bother you."

The four children settled down to wait – and to talk about the amazing place they had come to.

"I've heard stories about the forest city, but I

never imagined it would be anything like this," said Mbe. "Did you see that great ditch?"

Nosa nodded.

"Now I want to meet my father, more than ever."

Ada looked across the compound to the crowded street, just visible through the doorway. She thought about Papa Eze, Mama Ginika and the village where she'd lived her whole life, and it seemed suddenly very small.

****

They rested all day. Then, when it was dark, Amenze returned.

He led the children out

"We must go quickly. The guildsmen are waiting."

Chapter Twenty Two

A brave decision

"Welcome Nosa and Ada – and your young friends – " an old man gestured towards the children " – rarely do we meet in the darkness like this. But tonight Amenze has called us together for a special reason."

"Thank you, master of the woodcarvers' guild," said Amenze, rising from his seat.

There were many of them, grey haired like Amenze, and the light from the oil lamps, flickering on their faces made them look like stern carvings of gods.

Amenze turned towards the man seated on his other side.

"And greetings to Chief Efe of the Edionisen. We are honoured that you join us."

The man, who was more finely dressed, did not speak, but raised his hand and nodded solemnly.

Amenze continued.

"These are the children I told you about, Akele's lost son and daughter. These are the ones hunted by Chief Obiro. See – this is the very gift made by the head of my own guild, many years ago."

They all looked towards Ada now – to the armlet.

"Hold it up, Ada," said Amenze gently. And she did, raising her arm so that the bright metalwork shone in the light of the flames.

"See, Chief Efe? Guildsmen? This charm was blessed by the priestess at the shrine of Ogun on the day it was given to the young queen."

"I remember it," said the wood carver. "She looked so beautiful."

Others around the group nodded.

"And we all know about the sadness that followed," continued Amenze. "But I believe the sad times are now ending."

A murmur went around the room, more nodding.

"It may be so," said Chief Efe lifting his hand.

Everyone turned to him. His voice was grave.

"But what would you have me do? Our Ogiso trusts Chief Obiro as a great warrior."

"But who will he accuse next? Who else will be condemned by his lies?" Amenze protested. "No one is safe. This man threatens us all – even as he spins his lies, his eyes threaten anyone who stands in his way."

The large man at the end – the master ivory carver – suddenly stirred and stamped his foot on the ground.

"Day by day he gets richer – while we obey our Ogiso's laws and trade only through the proper channels. And no one is safe. Amenze is right!"

A silence settled on the room, as each man looked into his own thoughts. Ada watched them, feeling each breath, and each beat of her pulse. Beside her, she sensed her brother was feeling the same.

Then at last Chief Efe looked up.

"Very well, guildsmen. Tomorrow. Each of you go back to your guilds. Look in your workshops and speak to your people – find the best gifts you have for our Ogiso."

He stood, gathering the finely woven red shawl around his shoulders.

"It is time to act. Bring all your gifts to the palace. And bring the children too."

****

Far out, beyond the streets, the houses and courtyard gardens, the sun dipped below the trees into the forest.

And in that fading moment, between day and night, two weary warriors entered a room in the royal palace and knelt before their chief.

"Well? What news do you bring?"

"The children of Queen Akele – they have vanished, my chief. We almost caught them at the great river but they used some enchantment."

Chief Obiro snorted and stared down at them.

"Enchantment?"

"Yes, we swear it, great chief. We followed them across the lands until they disappeared. We could find no trail."

"Fools! Do you think that you are my only spies?

I already know what you came here to tell me."

The warriors glanced nervously at each other.

"Chief?"

Obiro was turning a knife in his hand, testing its edge on his thumb.

"You failed. The children are already here in the city, with Amenze. And now all the guildsmen are plotting against me."

Now he was on his feet, gesturing with the blade.

"But no matter. They will fail of course. Tomorrow I will speak to the Ogiso and I will warn him of great danger. I will tell him there can be no more glory in war, no more victories, unless he condemns those children, as he condemned their mother. And when I tell him that – " with a sudden jerk he threw the knife at the wall, and it stuck fast, quivering " – as always, the Ogiso will believe me."

Chapter Twenty Three

The sky-king

The sun was rising bright above the city and sweet morning smells of frying bean cakes filled the streets.

Amenze walked ahead, with Nosa and Ada following. Mbe and Madu, who were staying behind, watched them disappear into the crowd.

The city was bustling with life.

The road widened and they were pushing their way through a crowded marketplace, overflowing with traders – women with stacks of new pottery, weavers unfolding bright cloths to display their patterns in the sun, smiling merchants showing off new found treasures from lands beyond the forest, and young farmers with their fresh crops brought into the city that morning.

Suddenly the buildings became grander. The

people they passed were no longer ordinary workers, but wealthy merchants, warriors and chiefs.

And then straight ahead was a high, red wall.

The palace.

"Do not fear," said Amenze. "Your ancestors will be watching over you when you meet your father. This will be a glad day."

And he led them in through the gate.

****

"Today, many gifts have been laid at the sky-king's feet. But I am told that you have brought something strange Master of Iron."

The Ogiso sat on low rectangular stool. And beside him, on their smaller seats, sat Chief Efe and the other four men of the Edionisen

Amenze bowed.

"I have been blessed my chief. I have found the sky-king's lost children."

Kneeling behind him, Ada hardly dared raise her eyes to where her father sat. On either side, guards stood holding the symbols of royal power, the leaf-shaped eben and the curve-bladed ada.

Ada had an impression of quiet power and it reminded her faintly of Chief Iwe.

But whereas Chief Iwe had sprawled on his stool, fanned by feathers and waited on by servants, the Ogiso sat upright and unmoving, as silent as the men at his side.

And the Ogiso seemed more powerful for it. His presence filled the space.

"Are these the children?" he asked, his voice steady and deep.

"Yes, great king," replied Amenze. "They were saved from death when Queen Akele was condemned. They were born in the forest and survived. And when Chief Obiro sent his men to hunt them down, they were saved again. They are only children as you see – but they are the flesh and blood of their great father, and they ran for many days with hunters on their heels, and survived great dangers – "

Now Amenze gestured for the two of them to step forward. Nosa went first, kneeling before the king and Ada followed.

The Ogiso leaned forward slightly, his red

necklace shifting but his expression impassive.

"And they survived," continued Amenze. "Until at the edge of our great forest, the god delivered them safe to me. See, this is the armlet that was blessed at Ogun's shrine, made for Queen Akele – it has protected them."

For a long while nobody spoke and Ada felt the stillness of the room bearing down.

Then, daring to raise her eyes, she saw the Ogiso make a small gesture with his hand – at which Chief Efe, who was beside him, leaned in close to hear his words, softly spoken.

After a moment the chief straightened.

"The sky-king wonders: if Ogun's armlet protected the children, why did it not protect their mother?"

Amenze bowed again, searching for words.

"I am a simple craftsman great king... I cannot know the will of all the gods... but when evil is done..."

The Ogiso held up his hand.

"Enough."

And he suddenly stood. Without another

glance at the children, he left the room, his guard following.

When they had gone, the chief turned to Amenze.

"The sky-king will now hear what Chief Obiro has to say. You have made serious accusations against him Amenze, and we the Edionisen must discuss this. Judgement will be passed at sunset. For if one side is innocent, then another must be guilty. Follow me. I will show you where to wait."

****

They were led through the palace in silence. Ada's mind was racing, trying to make sense of what had just happened. She hardly noticed the rooms they were passing through.

Beyond the court room was an enclosed garden, with more openings leading from it. The chief took them through one room, then another.

Then he stopped beside a doorway.

"Children, you wait in here. Amenze, come with me."

Ada followed Nosa into the room.

And it was a moment before she realised they were not alone. There was somebody else waiting too, looking out through an opening to gardens beyond.

It was the Ogiso.

Chapter Twenty Four

A second meeting

"Seeing you is both a joy and a pain," the Ogiso said. "Your faces remind me of your mother."

He beckoned them forward.

"Come. Do not be afraid. I am the sky-king. But in this room, I am also your father."

Nosa bowed.

"Thank you sir."

"Sit with me. Both of you."

As they did, palace workers entered with bowls of fruit, and laid them out before the king.

"Now we will eat together," said the Ogiso. "And you will tell me your stories."

****

Nosa spoke first. The Ogiso listened, nodding from time to time, as the boy described his life at Chief Iwe's, growing up, not knowing his real family.

"I always dreamed of escaping to the forest," he said. "But I did not know where I would go."

"Your strength and courage does you credit."

"Thank you sir."

He turned to Ada.

"And now my daughter, what of you? Is this the charm of which I have heard?"

"Yes sir."

He looked thoughtfully at the armlet, as if remembering his past life.

"It is a great treasure indeed. And I hear it was kept safe for you – by a herbalist?"

"Yes. His name is Papa Eze. He raised me as his daughter."

The Ogiso nodded.

"Was he a good father? Did he treat you well?"

"Yes sir."

"Then he shall have my thanks."

He paused for a moment, as if gathering his

thoughts.

"So what is to happen next, my son and daughter?"

He sighed.

"You have seen that I have great power. But perhaps there is something that you do not see – I also carry a great burden. Many burdens, in truth."

He stood now, looking out at his city.

"I have ruled for many years and fought off many enemies. I have sacrificed to the gods to keep our land fertile. My city has grown and my people have prospered.

"And I am blessed with many wives, and many children.

"But there are always disputes to settle, arguments between powerful people. Always, I have to watch for new dangers.

"A king must listen to his chiefs. This man – Chief Obiro – he is a great hunter and warrior. He has many wives and sons. And many times he has been proven right and won battles for our people."

He turned back to them and laid his hands gently on both their shoulders.

"So I must hear what Chief Obiro has to say again today. It is my hope that you can stay here with me and help to build our city. But the will of the gods must be heard. I cannot let my feelings as a father cloud my judgement as a king."

****

He walked to the door, and with each step it seemed to Ada is if he were becoming more remote, becoming the sky-king again and ceasing to be their father.

And as he reached the door, Ada looked down.

She looked at the armlet on her wrist, and she felt it again – that sudden sense of urgency.

A thought came to her.

It was the memory of a story told to her by Papa Eze, long ago.

She remembered it, the tale of a girl who was trapped by a hungry leopard. Papa had even laughed and said that her name was Ada – she had escaped, not by speed or power, but by outwitting the hunter.

"Sir," she called out suddenly. "May I make a request?"

The Ogiso turned, puzzled.

"A request? What is it child?"

And pausing at the doorway he listened – half as king, half as father – as she explained her idea.

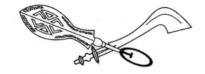

Chapter Twenty Four

A test of truth

Chief Obiro arrived last.

The five king-makers of the Edionisen had already taken their seats at the front of the king's hall, with all the elders and the head guildsmen gathered behind, talking in low voices.

Then Amenze and the children were led in, and everyone turned to look at them. Space was made in front of the sky-king's seat, and Ada felt their curious gazes – *who were they, this girl and boy?*

"Don't be afraid," Amenze whispered. "Stand straight."

Then the Ogiso himself entered, followed by four of the tallest warriors Ada had ever seen. Silence settled

And Chief Obiro arrived.

As he pushed his way through the crowd Ada felt her heart pounding.

Here he was, the man who had been hunting her, the man who had condemned her mother.

He looked strong, his body lean and battle scarred.

And now he was just a few steps away, bowing before the king.

He straightened, raising his arms. And she saw that he was holding something in his clenched fist.

Everyone waited.

"Gods protect you, great sky king," Chief Obiro said, kneeling.

The Ogiso nodded.

"What news do you bring, trusted war-chief?"

"That your enemies tremble beyond the forest, great king," he replied. "That your crops will grow, your people will prosper and wealth will flow into your land."

A satisfied murmur ran around the hall.

The Ogiso nodded.

"Then we are pleased."

Chief Obiro raised his voice.

"But my king, beware! A great evil has tried to come into our city – even here, among us!"

The hall was silent suddenly and the elders began to look at each other.

"A great evil? What evil do you speak of?"

Chief Obiro stood and pointed at the children.

"Great king – the gods are warning me again, just as they did in the past. These two are the children of the cursed Queen Akele! Amenze has brought them here in secret. He wants to gain power over your kingdom – and bad luck will befall your land again!"

An angry protest errupted, until the Ogiso raised his hand for silence.

"The gods warned you of this?"

"Yes, in a dream great king. I do not claim to be a diviner. But still I have many gifts which I have often used to keep the kingdom safe. And the same power that has guided me to victory so many times has told me what to do – to keep your land safe, to ensure future victories, the children must be sacrificed. And Amenze must be condemned too, for his treachery. He must die with them."

He unclenched his fist, to reveal a gourd, stained with black dye.

"They must take the poison!"

****

The Ogiso gestured, and two of his guards stepped forward.

Then he nodded to Chief Efe, who exclaimed:

"Chief Obiro – before he passes judgement, the sky-king wishes to know, are you sure this is really true? Are the gods speaking?"

"Yes my lord, and not just speaking – they are showing me the sign of death on these wicked children."

He glared down, and Ada shivered under the intensity of his gaze.

"The god Ogiuwu is calling their names. Nosa and Ada, cursed son and daughter of a cursed mother – " his voice became a growl. "I see the arms of Ogiuwu reaching for them – the underworld claims them!"

And nobody in the hall moved – nobody breathed – as he grabbed the two children and forced them to their knees.

"You are wrong. And you lie!" a voice shouted.

182

The crowd parted suddenly at the back of the hall, and a tall boy pushed forward, his eyes blazing.

"That is not Nosa, the sky-king's son. I am Nosa! The boy you hold is called Mbe. He is a farmer's son."

"What?"

"Are you surprised Chief Obiro? Did the gods not tell you?"

Chief Obiro stared, astonished – and the hall erupted in a riot of protest.

"What trickery is this?" Chief Obiro demanded. "What wickedness?" but his words were lost in the noise.

And then the Ogiso himself was standing.

****

"Chief Obiro. Why did you not recognise my son? You claimed the gods themselves were guiding you."

The hall fell silent.

"Speak."

Chief Obiro blustered, searching for words.

"Great king this…this is a mistake. This is

trickery…"

"No trickery. Simply a test. And you failed."

He nodded. Now his men seized the warrior's arms – he was strong, but they were younger and stronger.

"Wait, great king! The god Ogiuwu is my protector! He will demand a sacrifice…"

The king seized the curve-bladed ada from his herald, pointing it now at Chief Obiro.

"Then Ogiuwu shall have what he demands. Guards! Take him."

Chief Obiro was dragged from the hall, his protests fading – and in the stunned silence that followed the Ogiso turned and stretched out his arms.

"My children. Come forward."

Then Nosa and Ada were pushed forward together.

And around them the elders signalled their approval, as they were embraced by the sky-king.

Amenze stepped back, to stand with the other guildsmen.

And in the crowd, little Madu squeezed through

to reach Mbe and hug him.

"You did it," he said. "You tricked him! Were you scared?"

"Yes," Mbe replied. "Very scared. Were you?"

"No. I thought it was fun."

And they both started laughing.

****

Then suddenly, a change came over the room. Men were rushing about, orders were being shouted and the king himself swept out, followed by his guards with their swords drawn.

A warrior led Nosa out, with Mbe.

Ada felt a hand wrapping around hers – it was Madu – and then Chief Efe called them both to follow him.

He took them through the palace to a hidden garden.

"One of my wives will stay with you. You must keep out of sight."

"Why? What's happening?" asked Ada.

"This is a moment of great danger," the chief replied. "Obiro was a powerful man with many

185

sons. Our king must act swiftly to prevent trouble."

****

Much later, Ada learnt what happened.
Her father, the Ogiso, led his guards
across the city, straight to Obiro's compound. The
chief's high-walled building had almost as many
rooms as the royal palace itself.

A great crowd had already gathered there,
and now the people backed away as the Ogiso
approached – most of them knelt to him, but not
all. In front of the compound gates, Chief Obiro's
own sons and brothers stood together, fully armed.

Beside them, grey haired veterans were watching
on. They had followed Chief Obiro into many
battles.

But still, the greater numbers were with the
Ogiso.

His own guards lined up either side of him,
swords drawn and shields raised, and all the time
more men were hurrying in from their posts at the
great defensive bank.

For a moment it seemed as if the whole city and

even the rainforest was holding its breath.

Then the sky-king stepped into open the space.

He raised his ada, and when he spoke, his voice carried through the crowd to the very back.

"Warriors of Edo – word has reached me. Our forest border is threatened. Today I go myself to drive back our enemies. Come! The ancestors are watching!"

And without waiting for a reply, he walked through the crowd and out of the city – and men from both sides followed. Obiro was forgotten.

****

Ada learnt of all this from Chief Efe's first wife.

"The danger has passed," she said. "You can stay with my family tonight."

"But what about the enemies at the border?"

But the woman just chuckled.

"Do not fear them. The sky-king knows what he is doing."

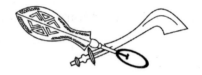

Chapter Twenty Five

The young warriors

For Mbe, the next days raced by like a strange, vivid dream. He was running beside Nosa through the rainforest again, following the twisting paths – but now it felt nothing like the journey of before. Then, they had been fleeing for their lives, now they were part of a fast moving army, being swept along as if on a flood.

He had never run so fast, or felt so full of life.

The youngest warriors were racing ahead of them now, keen to clear the way for the Ogiso and his great chiefs.

Nosa had been given a fine umozo sword of his own, and he was sprinting in full Edo war gear – but when he was called to join with all the king's sons in the royal guard, he grabbed Mbe's arm.

"Come with me Mbe," he whispered. "You are as much my brother as they are."

****

So Mbe found himself right near the front of the Edo army, when the warriors lined up at the forest edge, swords raised, to look out across the savannah.

In the heat of midday, Chief Iwe and his followers were approaching – at first nothing but shimmering dots, but soon resolving into men.

Iwe did not look so grand now and, among all his people, none carried any weapons. They had come to offer tribute. Iwe watched on anxiously as his men laid many gifts on the ground and waited.

After a long pause, the Ogiso himself emerged from the trees. And it seemed to Mbe that Iwe was trembling as he knelt down to pledge his loyalty.

"Never dare to enter our forest again," said the sky-king, his voice soft. "The next time I appear before you, I will not be merciful."

****

And then it was over, and Mbe was following the army back towards the city, jogging now not sprinting.

Beside him, Nosa was talking excitedly, going over again and again what had just happened, and making plans for the future.

"We will be great warriors," he laughed, putting his arm on Mbe's shoulder. "Hey, and you must get an Edo sword…"

Mbe laughed too – but he was thinking about Ada, and how far the two of them had come since leaving their village.

And he was wondering what would happen next.

Chapter Twenty Six

The ancestors

Ada watched the Ogiso's army return. From first light, crowds had gathered at the great defensive earth bank – the ironsmiths, the potters, the market traders, the farmers, the white-haired elders, the merchants, the children with their mothers and aunts – all jostling on top of the bank and lining the road into the city.

And when the sky-king appeared at last, ahead of his warriors, a great cheer went up. It reverberated through the forest and echoed back with the shrieks of startled birds.

And drum beats rose up in the city.

News of the Ogiso's triumph spread through the crowd – how the enemy had cowered before him! – and the people flowed behind his army into the city. Ada was swept along with them.

But in all that joyous throng she felt alone.

She had spent days in the palace, looked after by Chief Efe's wives.

But there was little for her to do, and she only felt cheerful when Madu visited her each day to tell her about the new things he had discovered. He was staying with Amenze in the metalworkers' quarter, and he was allowed to come and see her each evening.

"Don't worry Ada," he said. "Your brother and Mbe will be back soon."

But two days after the army returned, there was still no sign of them.

****

On the third day, Ada was invited to join some of the palace women who were weaving.

"It will be good for you to learn," said Chief Efe's wife.

"Yes Ma, thank you," Ada replied – and she did not say that Mama Ginika had already taught her everything she needed to know about cloth making.

She settled down with a loom in one of the

gardens – and looked up startled when she saw the women around her bowing.

The Ogiso was standing over her, holding out his hand.

"Come daughter."

****

"The last time we spoke, your wisdom surprised me," he said.

He was leading her through a passage that wound through to the back of the palace.

"For some time I had been troubled by my war chief, Obiro – he was a good servant once, but his power was growing too great. Your plan to test him was a wise one."

"Thank you my Ogiso…"

"But now – " he stopped and looked down at her. "What do you wish daughter? For your life?"

"Sir…?"

"When you were growing up, far from our forest, you wondered about your ancestors I believe. There was no shrine to them in your village."

She shook her head.

"The shrine is here," he said, pointing towards a doorway. "Here you may speak to your mother's spirit – I think she will answer you now…"

Ada looked uncertainly at the doorway. The room beyond was in shadow.

"Do not be troubled daughter. She will be proud of you."

The Ogiso stepped back.

"And then, when you are ready, you can decide."

"Decide?"

"Yes – what life will you live? If you wish, you can stay here in the palace, the daughter of the sky-king. You have many sisters and brothers here and you will never have want for anything. Or perhaps – perhaps you would prefer another life, the life you had before. The herbalist was kind, I have been told…"

He gestured towards the doorway.

"There is no hurry to decide. I will wait."

Ada felt herself trembling as she walked forward, into the half-darkness.

And once more, she felt the armlet smooth and warm against her skin.

She knelt and closed her eyes. And in that moment it seemed that she felt her mother's blessing – her pride in her daughter and her joy, despite sorrow at their life together lost.

Long moments passed before Ada stood again, wiping tears.

She had decided.

She knew what she wanted.

She turned to speak to the sky-king. But he was gone.

It was Mbe waiting there.

And leaning on his arm was an old traveller, wrapped in a shawl – Papa Eze had found her again, just as he'd promised.

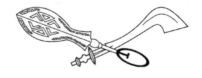

Fact vs Fiction

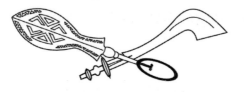

The real story of the Benin Kingdom

Was there really a powerful Edo kingdom in the rainforest?

Yes there was. Over a thousand years ago, in what is now southern Nigeria, the Edo people began to clear ground in the tropical rainforest where they lived.

Over time many small Edo villages joined together and gradually formed a large community, united under one leader.

This process was already well under way by the 12th century, the time when our story is set.

By then, a thriving community had become established, known as Igodomigodo.

It was named after a ruler called Igodo, who is said to have been the first king of the Edo people.

Why is this story called *Children of the Benin Kingdom?*

Today the ancient Igodomigodo civilisation is often referred to as the Benin Kingdom, and the forest city is called Benin City.

But the word 'Benin' would not have been recognised by the people of the 12th century, so we have used terms such as 'Edo kingdom' and 'forest city'.

To reflect modern usage, we have still used 'Benin' in our book title.

Note: the modern day country, the Republic of Benin, is located further to the east, and should not be confused with the medieval kingdom.

Was the Edo civilisation isolated in the rainforest?

Igodomigodo was not an isolated civilisation cut off in the rainforest. And nor was it particularly unusual in West Africa at this time.

In fact it was one of a series of kingdoms and empires that arose in the region from the 400s to the 1700s.

Many of these communities became sophisticated centres of art, where work of exceptional quality came to be produced in clay, wood, metal and ivory.

And these great centres of power were well known to one another – through trade, through the exchange of ideas and traditions, and sometimes through war.

Why are there pictures of cowrie shells on the cover of this book?

The cowrie shell was a widely accepted currency, used for buying and selling everything from crops to craftworks. Other currencies were accepted too, including glass beads. Like the cowries these had value because they were hard-wearing and relatively rare.

By the time our story is set, trading between the West African kingdoms, and right across to east Africa and beyond, had been an important part of life for centuries.

In our story, Mama Ginika and Chief Iwe are both skilled at trading with neighbouring peoples and dealing with merchants from further afield too. Idris (mentioned in chapter 7) is an Arab merchant.

This trade was made easier by the region's extensive network of rivers which enabled people to transport goods, and to travel quickly from one area to another, just as Ada and Mbe do in our story.

What were the symbols of power used by the Ogisos?

Although the Edo people had united under one Ogiso (or sky-king) the elders of the original villages still retained authority amongst their communities.

Part of the Ogiso's job was to ensure that these men would continue to support him and accept him as their leader.

As with any monarchy, the Ogiso had special symbols of power to impress people and to help him retain authority. You will find mention of some in our story:

• In artworks, the depiction of leopards was often associated with royal power.

• The 'ada' and 'eben' were emblems of royal authority that could only be owned with express permission from the sky-king. The ada is a curved blade, a ceremonial version of the Edo umozo sword. The eben is a leaf-shaped sword.

You can find graphic representations of ada and eben at various places in this book, including below.

• The colour red was associated with power in the Edo civilisation and the Ogiso probably wore red beads as symbol of authority. In later years the Obas (who succeeded the Ogisos as kings) wore red beads made of coral.

• The Ogiso sat on a special stool, an 'agba' to denote his authority and power.

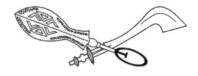

Who were the king-makers?

The Ogiso was supported by his council of Edionisen: five senior men who were hereditary chiefs within the kingdom. These advisers were the 'king-makers'. Their job was to support the sky-king in ruling Igodomigodo. They even had the power to overrule a king if it was felt that he was not making good decisions for the kingdom.

In our story, Chief Efe is a member of the Edionisen.

To help protect his rule, the king would also appoint warrior chiefs – some to keep order within the kingdom and some to fight wars with neighbouring peoples. Through such wars rulers could try to extend their kingdoms, and therefore their power and wealth. Warrior chiefs were very important. In our story, Chief Obiro is one such powerful man.

Were the guilds really important?

The ivory-carvers, iron-workers, wood-carvers and the other craftspeople were organised by the king into specialist groups, or 'guilds'.

The guild members lived and worked close to one another, with each guild occupying its own area of the city.

In our story, Amenze is the guild master of the blacksmiths, making him an important figure in the city.

The guild system was set up by the rulers as one way to keep control over the production of important items, such as tools and weapons.

Tools were essential for efficient farming and hunting, which was required to feed the large numbers of people in Igodomigodo. Good weapons were needed for protecting and enlarging the kingdom. And fine artworks were important for ceremonial and religious purposes.

Without books, how did knowledge spread?

Knowledge and traditions were not only shared among the members of each guild but also, sometimes, with craftspeople from other communities and kingdoms.

For example, Ogun, the god of iron, was not just worshiped in Edo culture, but in other cities.

One of the most important of these places was Ife, an influential city to the north of Igodomigodo. You can find Ife on the map at the beginning of this book – like Igodomigodo it is also a forest city.

Ife was influential in the development of artistic work and culture in Igodomigodo. In our story, specialists from Ife are seen sharing skills with Edo craftspeople (read carefully and you might spot this in the scene at the end of chapter six).

The Edo also shared knowledge through oral tradition and through visual representation in art, (for example, see the Benin Bronzes page 210).

What happened to the Ogisos?

The power, wealth and influence of Igodomigodo continued to grow into the 1400s. By this time the kingdom was one of the most important in West Africa. Throughout the 1400s and the 1500s the city was producing exceptional art which is evidence of its thriving culture.

The dynasty of the Ogisos came to an end in some time in the 1200s. Then a new dynasty, the Obas, took control and continued many of the same traditions.

This dynasty is still in existence today, with ceremonial and local power and patronage in Benin City, in the Edo State in Nigeria, which is where the Edo people still live.

It was during the 1400s that Igodomigodo began to be known (to outsiders) as 'Benin' and its capital began to be known as Benin City.

What are the 'Benin bronzes'?

Some of the most famous of the works of art produced during the kingdom's heyday are now known as the Benin Bronzes, many of which displayed in museums in Europe and the US.

The bronzes were used to adorn the Oba's palace and they were decorated with scenes from Benin history – they would have shone brightly in the sun and impressed visitors to the palace, reminding them of the power of the king.

The bronzes (which are actually made of brass and copper) were created over period of a few hundred years and were commissioned by the kings to record royal events. They portray a visual history of the kingdom. In addition to other events, the bronzes depict the arrival of Portuguese traders, who sailed from Europe to trade with the Edo people in the late 1400s.

Benin's famous city walls were built up during

The real story of the Benin kingdom

this period too – in our story they are described as earth banks and ditches but they were to become larger and more impressive over the following centuries.

By the 1600s they were significant structures extending to around 150 kilometres.

During the same period the city itself became larger and more sophisticated, with features such as roads paved with potsherds and oil lamps being used for street lighting.

The bronzes were stolen by British armed forces in 1897. During an attack much of the city was destroyed and the kingdom was subsequently forced to become a British colony. Benin city is now the capital of Edo State, Nigeria.

Which gods are mentioned in our story?

In traditional Edo religion, Osanobua is the creator of the world and the father of all the gods. Osanobua does not concern himself with human affairs, but sometimes his children, who are also gods, do.

These children of Osanobua are therefore worshipped at shrines – in the belief that they can affect what happens to humans. Osanobua's most important children are Olokun, Ogiuwu, Osun and Ogun. Olokun is the god of the rivers, water and wealth. Ogiuwu is the god of death. Osun is the god of medicine and healing.

Ogun is mentioned several times in our story. He is the deity of metalworkers and those who use metal, such as hunters.

In our story, Amenze stops at a shrine to Ogun, to pay his respects.

The Ogisos were also believed to be descended from Osanobua and were thought to be semi-divine. This is why they were called the 'sky-kings'.

The acceptance of their divine right to rule helped to maintain their authority. The Ogisos took care to preserve this belief.

Why are ancestors important in the story?

In common with other peoples in the region, the Edo believed in the importance and power of their ancestors, who reside in the spirit world. Shrines to ancestors would be located in homes, and appeals for help would be addressed to the ancestors, as well as to the gods. Ancestors would watch over families, could help with problems and sometimes could create trouble for the living if they were angry.

In our story, Ada is worried about not knowing her ancestors.

What is the role of divination and traditional medicine?

The Edo system of divination, in common with others across the region, is believed by followers to offer help with life's problems, including illnesses and difficult decisions.

Sometimes diviners try to find answers by interpreting the way that objects fall when they are cast on the ground, combining that with their knowledge of proverbs, folklore and history.

In our story, Ujo uses four strands, each containing seeds. Ujo throws, or casts, these onto the ground.

In traditional practice, a diviner might look at which side up the seeds land (there are many combinations) and use this to interpret the cause of a person's problems, and to offer advice on what they should do.

Some diviners specialise in medical matters only and these are more akin to Papa Eze – medical herbalists who aim to use their specialist knowledge to treat physical illnesses.

Papa Eze is a herbalist healer only.

Many herbalists and healers would have combined their knowledge of folklore, charms and incantations, along with their understanding of the properties of plants, to offer treatments to patients.

Diviners, herbalists and religious specialists, such as priests and oracles, can all offer to cure ailments and their skills often overlap.

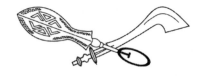